'For such a small and peaceful-looking island it does seem extraordinarily subject to turmoil and violence of one sort or another,' he commented. 'Passions clearly run very high hereabouts.' He caught Lorna's eye and she grinned.

'Ah, well, we Celts are an ancient and passionate race,' she said, glancing up at him.

Martin raised one eyebrow. 'So I've noticed,' he remarked drily. 'And just to put the record straight, I also lay claim to Celtic blood and can be as passionate as the next man—or woman—when I'm roused.'

There was a short, pregnant pause and Lorna kept her head studiously turned away as her fingers struggled with the buckles of her sandals. Was his remark a warning—or a promise? His tone gave nothing away, but this certainly wasn't the moment to put it to the test.

Another book you will enjoy
by HELENA DAWSON

PORTRAIT OF A STRANGER

Charlie was convinced that her next commission was going to launch her career as an artist—until she discovered that her eminent subject, Calum Sutherland, was none other than the businessman she had antagonised earlier, and was as disagreeable and narrow-minded as ever!

RIGHT CONCLUSIONS

BY

HELENA DAWSON

MILLS & BOON LIMITED
ETON HOUSE 18-24 PARADISE ROAD
RICHMOND SURREY TW9 1SR

All the characters in this book have no existence outside the imagination of the Author, and have no relation whatsoever to anyone bearing the same name or names. They are not even distantly inspired by any individual known or unknown to the Author, and all the incidents are pure invention.

First published in Great Britain 1991
by Mills & Boon Limited

This edition 1991

ISBN 0 263 77193 8

Set in Times Roman 10 on 12 pt.
01-9108-53120 C

Made and printed in Great Britain

CHAPTER ONE

'WELL, I think it's great news, just what the island needs, and the sooner they start, the better—oh, sorry, Lorna, I didn't see you standing there!'

Lorna stood aside, smiling, to let Mrs Ogilvie through the shop door, still talking over her shoulder to the other women by the counter.

'It could help your Jimmy to get a job here, Jean, instead of having to try to find work on the mainland.'

'Jimmy and the rest of the youngsters,' Jean Mair agreed.

Lorna shut the door behind Mrs Ogilvie and crossed over to join the other women.

'What's the excitement about?' she asked. 'Who's starting what? Have I missed something?'

She could tell by the air of suppressed excitement that it was a piece of unusual news that they had all been discussing and she looked from one face to another, waiting for enlightenment. Jean Mair came to her rescue.

'You haven't heard, then?'

Lorna shook her head. 'I won't know till someone tells me.'

'Well——' the older woman laid a confiding hand on her arm '—apparently some big holiday firm from the mainland—Glasgow, I think—wants to build a . . . what do you call it, Mary?'

'A leisure centre,' Mary MacPherson informed her, 'and a marina, I think Jessie Kincaid said.'

'That's right.' Jean Mair nodded. 'With chalets, a heated swimming-pool—oh, I don't know, all sorts of attractions. A complete holiday village, in fact.'

Lorna looked into Jean's beaming face with a sickening feeling creeping up from the pit of her stomach. 'Where are they planning to build this . . . this village?' she asked.

Jean waved her hand vaguely. 'On the north coast, somewhere between Calgary and Dervaig, I think. It'd be near Croig, I imagine, by the old drovers' harbour.'

'Ay, it's about time someone did something about that,' Mary MacPherson put in. 'A real eyesore it is, and always has been.'

'A leisure centre and holiday village at Croig?' Lorna echoed weakly, unable to believe her ears. A vision swam before her of the quiet, sheltered beaches shattered by hordes of noisy holiday-makers, the coastline littered with chalets, the little ruined harbour demolished to make way for a plush new marina . . . 'Are you sure? It couldn't just be a rumour?'

'I may have got it wrong, but everyone's talking about it.' Jean straightened up from packing away her shopping and saw the bleak look on Lorna's face. 'I'd have thought you'd have been pleased, dear. It'll bring in a lot more business for us all, and, as Mrs Ogilvie said, youngsters like my Jimmy will be glad of the extra jobs a place like that will bring,' she ended firmly. She picked up her bag and moved off to the door. 'Ask Iain, he'll know all the details—he always knows what's going on.'

Lorna stared after her, then at Mary MacPherson. 'Where is Iain, anyway?'

'Out in the back, getting me some potatoes.' Mary paused, then pursed her lips. 'You don't think it'll be a good thing for the island, then?'

Lorna remembered just in time that Mary MacPherson's husband had been out of work since the island's one and only boat-building firm had gone out of business, and sighed.

'I suppose it might be, in one way. Of course the extra jobs would be welcome, I can see that, but just think of all the extra traffic, not to mention the pollution and the noise. Do we really want a sort of Scottish Disneyland on the island?'

Her heart sank even as she spoke, visualising only too clearly what such a development would involve. But Mary wasn't the person to try to explain her fears to. She peered beyond the counter through the open door that led to Iain's storeroom.

Where *was* Iain? He'd be on her side... They'd shared enough picnics on Croig beach over the past twenty-odd years for her to be sure of that.

A large figure emerged through the doorway holding a bulging bag of potatoes.

'There you are, Mrs MacPherson. Sorry to have been so long. Oh, hello, Lorna! How nice! I'll be with you in a minute.'

Lorna waited impatiently while Iain packed up Mary MacPherson's shopping for her, added up the bill and counted out her change before going to open the door for her, taking his time and chatting to her all the while about her family and neighbours until, by the time Iain had seen her on her way, Lorna felt she'd explode.

'At last! I thought she'd never go! Listen, Iain, what's all this about a holiday village near Croig? It's not true, is it? They've got it wrong, haven't they, Mrs Ogilvie and the others?'

She held tightly on to Iain's arm, searching his face anxiously. Frowning, Iain ran his hand through his hair.

'Mr Miller was telling me—he's on the council now, you know?'

'Yes, yes, I know...go on!'

'Well,' Iain continued with irritating slowness, 'there's not a lot to tell yet, but I gathered some holiday firm—I can't remember its name—has expressed an interest in the site; nothing more than that. There'll be miles of red tape to unravel before they can do anything—planning applications, site meetings...all that. Protests, too, I dare say,' he added with a grin as he took in the light of battle in Lorna's eyes.

'Of course there'll be protests,' she rejoined hotly, 'and it's no laughing matter, Iain MacDonald! I'd have thought that you, of all people, would have understood that. They can't be allowed to ruin the island without a struggle.'

'At least it would be hidden away, off the beaten track, if they built something there,' Iain pointed out. 'And, as Mrs Ogilvie was saying, we could do with the jobs here, as well as the extra business a place like that would bring in.'

Lorna stared open-mouthed at her old friend. 'Iain, *you're* not in favour of it, too? You can't be!'

Iain shrugged. 'You have to be realistic, Lorna, and money isn't exactly rolling in just at present. In fact...'

His pleasantly open face clouded as he stared round the shop, but Lorna was too preoccupied to notice.

'I'd rather be poor for the rest of my life than let the developers ruin the island,' she asserted fiercely, 'and I'd have thought you would have felt the same.'

'Lorna, let me explain...'

But Lorna wasn't in a mood to listen to explanations or to anything else Iain might have to say on a subject they clearly differed about so fundamentally. She marched over to the door and flung it open before glaring back at Iain who was left staring helplessly after her.

'I always thought we were on the same wavelength, Iain, but it's amazing how wrong you can be about people you've known all your life, isn't it?'

The door banged to behind her as Lorna clambered into the old Land Rover parked outside and slammed it into gear.

How could he, she muttered to herself, how could Iain, born and brought up on the island as she herself had been, go along with this dreadful proposal? How could he think that money was more important than safeguarding the beauty that lay all around them?

Her foot eased off the accelerator as she gazed out at the rolling moorland stretching away from the road, then pulled over on to the narrow grass verge and turned off the engine. Almost subconsciously she had brought herself to one of her very favourite places, a spot she seldom passed without taking time off to marvel at the view, always beautiful, and each time subtly different.

Today the air was still, warmed by a hazy sun that gave promise of a lovely day later on and bathed the familiar landmarks in a gentle glow; but sometimes, when a storm threatened, she had seen each leaf and blade of grass stand out in the livid light with an almost frightening clarity. And there were times, too, when the concealing veil of a sea mist would envelop the whole landscape, blotting out the shapes of the mountains across the Sound that today receded in ever paler shades of blue so that they appeared to float above the water.

Heathery moorland swept back from one side of the road, and on the other the sea lapped gently at the grass and shingle under her feet. There was no sign of human habitation visible from this point and no sound other than the occasional bleat of a distant sheep, or the twitter of a bird in the pines fringeing the shoreline.

Here was real peace, Lorna thought, feeling the pervading tranquillity begin to work its magic, and at least the holiday company hadn't cast their greedy eyes on this place—yet—and maybe she had rather jumped to the worst conclusions about the whole thing. After all, as Iain had reasonably pointed out, nothing had been decided yet, and so far as anyone could tell the holiday scheme was nothing but a gleam in the developer's eye. A lot could happen along the way...they might not even get planning permission at all. No point in getting worked up yet, just prepared.

It was odd about Iain, though. She'd have thought he of all people would want the island kept as they'd always known and loved it.

Lorna leant back against the Land Rover and stared out over the sea to the mainland with unfocused eyes, wondering about her old friend. He had been part of her life since her earliest childhood, and she would never have questioned the fact that they thought alike on almost everything—everything that mattered, anyway.

They had always been almost inseparable companions. Even when Lorna had gone away to study for her English degree at St Andrews, Iain had come over to partner her to university balls. He had always been the only man for her, just as the island was the only place where she ever wanted to live. Everyone, including Lorna herself, knew it was only a matter of time before they got married and settled down together.

With a little sigh that transformed itself into a rueful smile, Lorna shook herself out of her reverie. Iain couldn't have thought the thing through properly. He'd come round to her way of thinking when she'd had a chance to talk to him, but flouncing out of the shop hadn't been the best way to go about it.

She'd have to see what she could do to put things right between them when she went back to get the groceries she'd forgotten to pick up just now in her hasty departure.

And that was what she ought to do right now. It was all very well dallying here, drinking in the view, but there was work to be done.

With another, longer sigh, Lorna straightened up and gave herself a last, wistful look at the view, grateful that it had once again worked its never-failing magic on her, then, reluctantly, she climbed back into the Land Rover and set off back the way she'd come.

She pulled over on to the single-track road and set off for the village store, driving carefully to avoid the sheep she noticed sheltering beneath a large boulder only yards ahead.

'Don't cross yet,' she warned them with a grin, knowing their ways of old. People thought they were stupid animals, but they were wrong. Obstinately perverse and wayward they might be, but not stupid...

She slowed down to approach a corner, not really concentrating on the road she knew like the back of her hand as her mind strayed ahead to what she would say to Iain. He wasn't one to bear grudges, so gentle and forgiving a man——

'Oh, my goodness!'

A large car was approaching her very fast and right in the middle of the road, its horn blaring furiously.

'What's that fool doing?' Lorna cried out in panic as she jammed on the brakes. There was no escape and she sat with her eyes tight shut, hands clenched on the steering-wheel, bracing herself for the inevitable collision. But nothing happened.

Cautiously she opened her eyes to see the other car parked at a crazy angle only yards away and a big, very angry-looking man heading in her direction.

'What the hell d'you think you were doing, driving like that?' she heard him shout even before he reached her.

She turned wide green eyes on him as he tore over to her vehicle to lean one arm on the roof and bend down to accost her, the top half of his body filling the window space.

'Well, did you hear what I said?'

His voice was deeply resonant and commanding, and Lorna found herself staring into a pair of piercing blue eyes, forcing herself to meet their angry gaze as steadily as she could even as she fought to control the pounding of her heart as well as her rising temper.

'Yes, thanks,' she said, annoyed to hear her voice shaking. 'I heard you perfectly well, and there was nothing wrong with my driving. I was in fact taking more than usual care, watching out for those sheep.'

Lorna turned to point them out, but with typical uncooperativeness they had moved away, leaving no sign of their presence but a tuft of wool on a stem of grass.

'Well, they were there, I can assure you,' she asserted, 'and as I thought they might suddenly rush across, *I* was driving quite slowly. It was you who was driving too fast—much too fast for these roads.'

The man drew in a breath of outrage and Lorna pressed home her advantage before he could begin the tirade against women drivers she sensed was on his lips.

'I guess you're from the mainland,' she went on, silkily polite, 'or you'd know that this is a one-track road, like most of the roads on the island, and you are supposed to watch out for oncoming traffic and one of you pull into a passing-place—like that.' She indicated a slight widening of the road just beyond where his car had stopped.

'And how was I supposed to know that? We don't all have second sight, you know! And in any case,' the man persisted grimly, 'if you'd been concentrating properly, instead of looking at the wildlife, you'd have seen me in plenty of time to draw over yourself.'

They glared at one another through the Land Rover's open window and, although the stranger had definitely been in the wrong himself, Lorna felt her earlier advantage slipping away as she had to acknowledge the truth of what he had just said. Her mind hadn't been entirely on her driving.

Just then the man took a step back, giving Lorna her first proper view of him. She'd seen he was tall as he had covered the space between their two vehicles with a few long strides, but that he was quite so tall, well over six feet, she'd not registered.

He was slim for his height, but with broad shoulders emphasised by the cut of the elegant grey flannel suit he was wearing—much too elegant, she thought uncharitably, and quite out of place here, on a Hebridean island, as were his striped shirt and silk tie.

In fact, everything about him shouted 'city', from his inappropriate clothes to his expensively styled dark hair, and the more she looked at him the more she disliked what she saw.

A sardonic smile did little to alter her opinion.

'Quite obviously the transport system here has hardly moved into the twentieth century,' he said acidly, closing the gap between them again and tapping on the roof of her Land Rover with a sharp tattoo of his fingers.

'I wasn't aware that this was such a primitive backwater, but I shall certainly note the fact for future reference.'

He frowned and looked about him with exaggerated care. 'I'm surprised you don't have little old men with red lamps guiding the traffic,' he went on with heavy sarcasm, one eyebrow lifting arrogantly as he ran his eyes over the shabby Land Rover. 'But I don't think any harm has been done, at least not to your vehicle, as far as it's possible to tell. As for mine...'

Seething with pent-up fury, Lorna followed his gaze over to the shiny black saloon poised drunkenly on the grass verge. It was a Mercedes, and brand new, she judged from the number plate, but the only damage it had apparently suffered had been to its dignity.

'There doesn't seem to be anything wrong with it, does there?' she snapped. 'But if you find that there is, and you consider I am to blame,' she added, throwing caution to the winds, 'please don't hesitate to let me know. We're not so primitive here that we're outside the law. I am fully insured, I assure you.'

Her voice was beginning to tremble from the shock of their near-collision and the stranger's sustained attack, but she continued as steadily as she could, 'Lorna Morrison's my name, and anyone on the island will tell you where I live.'

An odd flicker gleamed momentarily in the stony sapphire gaze, but the man's voice remained as icy as before.

'I don't imagine that will be necessary, Miss——' he flashed a glance at her left hand '—Miss Morrison. But if I might say so, perhaps a smaller vehicle would suit you better. You might find it easier to control.'

He smiled pleasantly as Lorna drew in an infuriated breath and with a renewed effort of will she just managed to restrain the outburst hovering on her lips. Nothing would be gained by indulging in a slanging match—best to retire with some dignity.

'Thank you for your advice,' she said with steely politeness. 'I'll certainly bear it in mind, but I'm afraid I simply haven't the time to discuss it just at the moment. I can see that you are a *very* busy man, and I mustn't hold you up any longer.'

For an instant their eyes met and held like adversaries sizing one another up before a trial of strength, neither giving nor expecting any quarter; then, with a little nod, Lorna snapped her window across, forcing him to step smartly backwards, and turned her engine on to pull over on to the road. She revved up more noisily than she normally did and felt a certain malicious glee at the sound of the gravel spattering up behind her and probably hitting the Mercedes as she passed it.

That'll teach him, she thought, as she looked in her mirror for one final glance at the man left staring after her. Round one to me, I think!

She shot round the corner, but once out of sight she slowed down as a new thought struck her. Supposing there really had been some damage to his car, and he was left stranded there? It was a very quiet road, even by island standards, and it might be ages before anyone came past.

Lorna sat still, frowning. It went against the grain to admit it, but it had been partly—though a very small part—her fault that the other car had been forced off the road. She *might* have been able to take avoiding action if she hadn't been thinking about other things...

There was no harm in going back just to check. After all, she wouldn't need to stop, or even speak to him, and, in any case, in all probability he'd have disappeared by now.

But he hadn't, and although the car had been straightened up from its former undignified position, it hadn't been driven more than a couple of yards, and when its owner saw Lorna slow down beside him his expression was less than delighted.

'Miss Morrison?' The deep voice was harsh. 'Come back to gloat, have you? Well, you have every excuse for doing so, as you can no doubt see. I seem to be stuck here.'

Lorna pulled in just ahead of the big Mercedes and jumped down to go and stand by the dark stranger.

'Won't it start?'

She looked from the car up into his face, noting the aggressive set of his jaw and the firm mouth framed between deep lines running down from the sides of his straight nose.

'What does it look like? No, Miss Morrison, it won't. Or at least it will start, but something seems to have shaken loose underneath, and as it's brand new I don't want to take any risks with it, so unless there's a competent mechanic somewhere in this benighted place I suppose I'll have to get someone over from Glasgow to take a look at it. Goodness knows how.'

Sparks of frustration and irritation blazed from the brilliant blue eyes narrowed now beneath the heavy lids.

If only he'd stop glowering, Lorna found herself thinking, he'd really be extraordinarily attractive, and to her dismayed astonishment she felt an odd lurch somewhere in the pit of her stomach as his penetrating glance came to rest on her own upturned face.

In instinctive self-defence she took a step back and reached for the thick plait lying over her shoulder to twirl the end between her fingers.

'I may be able to help——' she began, but the man cut her off with a brusque laugh.

'I doubt it. A Mercedes has an extremely complicated engine.'

Lorna felt her cheeks grow warm, but went on steadily, 'I didn't mean *I* could fix it personally. Give me credit for some sense, please.' The man grunted what might charitably have been called an apology as Lorna continued, 'But I can give you a lift to the nearest garage, if you like? The owner, Archie McIntyre, is a good friend of mine, and if anyone can put it right he'll be able to. And if he can't, you can ring Glasgow from there.'

The man frowned.

'Hobson's choice, I suppose,' he muttered, turning to lock the doors. Lorna saw him pause for a moment before swinging round to face her again, his mind made up.

'If it's not too much trouble, then,' he said a fraction less aggressively, 'I'd be very grateful for your offer. My name's Ritchie, by the way. Martin Ritchie.'

He held out his hand with a wry twist to his lips and Lorna put hers into it, feeling, with a sense of shock, a tremor run up her arm, making goose-pimples stand out on her tanned skin.

For a second longer than was absolutely necessary for politeness's sake Martin Ritchie held her imprisoned, then, without another word, he released her to stride round to the passenger side of the Land Rover and climb up into the seat beside hers.

Lorna did her best to calm her accelerating heartbeat as she carefully reversed the unwieldy vehicle, painfully conscious of Martin Ritchie's unwavering stare. It wouldn't do to put a foot wrong with this particular passenger eyeing her so critically.

'Did you come back specially?' he asked after a short silence. 'I'm sorry; I shouldn't have suggested it was to gloat—that was hardly fair of me.'

Lorna felt his eyes still scanning her face, but kept her own resolutely on the road ahead.

'Yes, I did,' she admitted. 'It's a very quiet road, and I realised that if anything had gone wrong with your car it might be hours before you could get help.'

It occurred to her then for the first time that it was strange that Martin Ritchie, in his smart city suit and expensive car, should be travelling along that particular road at all. What was he doing there, and where could he have been going?

She allowed herself a brief glance across and was relieved to see that he was now staring straight ahead and not taking any notice of her.

'It's a pretty quiet place altogether, your island, isn't it? Not a lot going on here.'

'And that's how we like it,' Lorna replied shortly. 'And we intend to keep it that way, too,' she added.

Martin Ritchie turned at the bitter note in Lorna's voice, his eyebrows lifting in mute curiosity, then he shrugged and went back to his study of the deserted landscape. Local political squabbles, if his guess at the reason for Lorna's comment was correct, were nothing to do with him. He had problems enough of his own to worry about.

'This garage of yours,' he asked, 'is it far?'

'Only about another mile,' Lorna told him, manoeuvring the big vehicle deftly round a tractor and trailer parked by the side of the road. 'You haven't been to the island before, have you? Are you here on business? You don't look like a holiday-maker, if you don't mind my saying so.'

She grinned, but the response to her questions was cool.

'No, I haven't, and Yes to your second question. At least, that was the idea, but I can't see that I shall get much done if my car's out of action for any length of time.'

The firm lips clamped shut and Lorna suppressed a sigh. So much for her attempt at friendliness. She'd keep her own mouth shut for the rest of the journey, and stuck to her resolve even as she drove past the end of the track leading up to her own home.

She stole a quick glance at the dour profile beside her. No glimmer of interest in his surroundings lit the darkly brooding eyes, so Lorna left unexplained the sign which read, 'GLENMORE HOUSE. BED & BREAKFAST. PONY TREKKING. CRAFTS,' and pressed on as quickly as she dared to Archie McIntyre's garage.

'Here we are. I'll go and see if Archie's around, and you can tell him what you want him to do.'

Martin Ritchie gazed in disbelief at the ramshackle yard piled with disintegrating wrecks so rusted it was impossible to tell what they had once been.

'This is a garage? You expect me to trust my car to the man who runs this?'

Lorna opened her door and jumped down, flicking back her plait with a defiant lift of her chin.

'You won't find anyone better on the island, I assure you. Archie can fix anything—you'll see.'

She saw him glance again at the pile of old crocks and grinned at his expression.

'Don't worry. Your precious Merc won't end up there. If you think about it, it's pretty hard on an island to get rid of machinery, short of dumping it in the sea. Anything that might have usable parts ends up here, or at the other garages. Stay there, I won't be a sec.'

Martin Ritchie still looked unconvinced as she left him to make her way round to the workshop at the back, finding her quarry on his back beneath a car so comparatively new that she regretted that Martin Ritchie wasn't with her. It might have at least reassured him about Archie's credentials.

'You'll be all right now, then, Mr Ritchie?' she asked him as she prepared to leave the two men together. 'I must be off, I'm afraid. I do have a business of my own to run.'

Martin Ritchie nodded briefly. 'You've done more than enough already,' he said ambiguously, 'and it was good of you to give me a lift.'

He offered his hand and Lorna took it, her eyes widening in instinctive response to the hard, warm grasp of his fingers round hers.

His lips twitched. Had he read on her face what she'd rather not admit even to herself—that she was in grave danger of succumbing to this man's undeniable physical attractions? Lorna pulled her hand away quickly and thrust it into her jeans pocket.

'I'll be away, then,' she said rather gruffly, and turned to climb back into her Land Rover. To her surprise Martin Ritchie followed her round, holding the door open then closing it after her.

'Thanks again,' he said, a new note, almost of warmth, audible in the deep voice. 'And mind how you go. No more close encounters of a dangerous kind.'

The blue eyes held Lorna's in an enigmatic scrutiny which reawakened that unwelcome surge in the pit of her stomach so that the smile she gave him wasn't as casual as she would have liked.

'I'll try. You too, Mr Ritchie. Take care on our primitive roads, won't you, once your car is back on them, that is?'

Lorna was glad it wasn't far from Archie's garage to Glenmore and that there was no hyper-critical passenger beside her to witness her rather erratic driving; and it wasn't only the narrow escape from what might have been a very nasty accident that was affecting her concentration, she knew...

She was more than usually pleased to see Jane's old Escort parked in the stable-yard behind her house as she drove up. A friendly chat with someone sympathetic was what she felt she needed more than anything just at the moment.

She hurried over to the little shop they had set up together in what had been the old wash-house.

'Hi, there!' she called out. 'Any coffee going? It's been quite a morning, I can tell you, and the day's hardly started yet!'

'Oh?'

Jane glanced up interestedly as she went on with her job of arranging some new stock on the shelves. 'What's been going on? Just hang on while I finish this—unless you'd like to put the kettle on?'

'Well, I've just met this man,' Lorna told Jane through the doorway of the little room at the back which served as office, storeroom and kitchen. 'No, not *that* sort of man,' she laughed, noting Jane's expression, 'a thoroughly nasty one, in fact, and definitely not someone I want to run into again. Definitely,' she repeated more firmly. 'And "run into" are the operative words.'

'Tell me more,' Jane urged, perching on the edge of the counter; so, pulling up a stool and subsiding gratefully on to it, Lorna related all that had happened that morning, from her visit to Iain's shop until the moment she had left Martin Ritchie at Archie's garage.

'No wonder you needed that.' Jane grinned as Lorna drained the last drop of her coffee. 'Quite a saga, to say the least.'

Lorna rested her elbows on the counter, supporting her chin on her hands. 'What puzzles me is what Martin Ritchie was doing here at all. He looked so out of place—I mean, you just don't see men in city suits and silk ties shooting round the island in fast cars, do you? Where could he have been going? That's what I want to know.'

'Curiosity killed the cat.' Jane laughed, sliding down from the counter top to begin unpacking another carton. 'He could have been doing anything at all. Maybe he's something to do with the holiday village—here, what have I said?'

Lorna pushed back her stool with such ferocity that it fell over with a crash, and glared so fiercely at her friend that Jane cringed back in mock alarm.

'Of course—that's it, isn't it? Why didn't I think of that before? Then I'd have given him a piece of my mind. To think I had him there, just where he couldn't escape… Oh, how stupid can you get?'

She beat her fists in pure frustration against her thighs and began pacing round the shop.

'It all fits, doesn't it? Spying out the land, that's what he was doing, and probably on his way to making a deal with the owner of the land he has his greedy eye on. To think I actually offered him a lift, too! I should have left him stranded—for good!'

Jane peered at her more closely. 'Aren't you going a bit over the top, love? I mean, I know how much you love the island, and it must have been a shock finding out about the development, but if it's done imaginatively—well, it mightn't be such a bad thing. We could all do with some extra trade—even here.'

Lorna swung round to face her friend, disbelief written on every line of her face. 'You're not in favour of it, too? I thought you'd come here for the peace and quiet, to get away from all that development... For goodness' sake, don't any of my friends feel as I do?'

She flung away from Jane, who reached out a hand to pull her gently back. 'Here, don't go leaping to conclusions, Lorna Morrison! I never said I was in favour, only that I could see some advantages to bringing more visitors here.'

'You sound just like Iain,' Lorna said in disgust. 'He sat on the fence as well, and I'd never have thought it of him, and I told him so too, or as good as.'

'You fell out with Iain?' Jane glanced up quickly, her brown eyes bird-bright. 'You two never argue about anything.'

'There's a first time for everything.' Lorna shrugged resignedly with a rueful smile. 'Still, I dare say we'll make it up soon enough once I get him round to my way of thinking. Now, I suppose I'd better go and get on. It's a good job there's no ride booked in for this afternoon. Thanks to Mr Martin Ritchie, I'm miles behind with all I meant to do.'

CHAPTER TWO

'I DON'T know where the day's gone,' Lorna complained to Jane when they were locking up the shop later that day. 'With no rides booked, I'd planned to do so much, and what have I got to show for it?'

'A very fetching brown streak across your forehead, for a start!' Jane laughed. 'Have you been gardening?'

'I did a bit of weeding round the front, more for appearance's sake than anything. Mum would have a fit if she could see the state of the garden,' Lorna sighed, 'but keeping the vegetable patch going is about as much as I can cope with. Speaking of which, why don't you stay for supper? Nothing grand, but there are a whole lot of beans which need eating, and I could do some baked potatoes. How about it?'

'Sounds lovely, if you're sure,' Jane said enthusiastically. 'Though I'll have to go back home first. There's some work I want to finish. Oh, by the way, I took a phone message for you earlier. You've got a booking for this evening. I thought you said you weren't full, so I told them it was OK. I hope it was?'

'Yes, that's fine,' Lorna answered. 'I'd better go and clean up, then, and check the room. See you in an hour or so.'

She scrubbed some potatoes and put them into the oven to bake, and was halfway up the stairs to wash and change when there was a ring at the front door.

Bother, she thought. It couldn't be Jane back so soon, and, besides, she would come straight in through the back door. It could only be a bed-and-breakfast guest, probably the one who had booked in earlier, and although she was pleased to have the business she would have preferred them to have arrived just a little later, when she was ready.

The bell rang again, more peremptorily this time, and reluctantly Lorna came down and crossed the hall, rearranging her face into a welcoming smile as she slid back the latch.

'Good evening, can I help...? Oh, it's you!'

Her heart somersaulted as once again she found herself looking up into an all too familiar pair of astonishingly blue eyes.

'Good evening, Miss Morrison,' their owner said politely. 'I wonder if I might have a word?'

Lorna thought of all the words she'd promised herself she would say if she ever set eyes on Martin Ritchie again, but swallowed them back as she recovered herself quickly.

'I suppose you've come about your car? Was it damaged, after all?' She stood back, tacitly inviting him inside. 'If you'd like to come in I'll go and find my insurance documents——'

'No, no.' He cut her off impatiently with a swift movement of his hand. 'It is because of my car that I'm here—nothing to do with our...our confrontation this morning—but not directly.'

Lorna looked up at him expectantly, thrusting her hands deep into the pockets of her jeans, and noted absently that those piercing eyes she had first seen glaring at her through the window of the Land Rover, although still as penetrating, seemed to gleam a fraction less harshly now as he went on, 'I need somewhere to stay, and Archie McIntyre told me you do bed and breakfast here, so I rang earlier and someone, clearly not you, told me you had room.'

'Yes, that's right,' she admitted slowly, 'but I wasn't expecting——'

Again he interrupted her. 'So you are full up after all?' He peered disbelievingly round the empty hall. 'But if not, I was wondering whether it would be possible for me to have a room for a night or so? It seems my car's going to be off the road for at least that long.'

His brows drew together in an angry frown.

Lorna thought quickly, uncomfortably conscious of her stained jeans and crumpled shirt, to say nothing of the smudge of earth still no doubt smearing her face. Martin Ritchie, of course, looked as immaculately elegant as he had that morning.

What should she say? Heaven knew, the last thing she wanted—or would have expected—was to have to put this man up in her house, but she couldn't really afford to turn anyone away, whatever her personal feelings towards them.

'Well, have you a room, Miss Morrison? Because if not, I'll have to look somewhere else.' His fingers tapped impatiently on the door as he waited for her response. 'Is there some problem?' he asked lightly. 'Or do you always scrutinise your potential customers so closely before admitting them? I assure you I am the soul of honesty, as well as strictly honourable.'

Lorna's cheeks reddened. 'No, of course it's not that. It's just . . .' She stared helplessly at him, trying to think up some excuse for her prevarication, when a thought struck her that made up her mind for her. While he was staying here she might have an opportunity—no, she'd see she made one—to find out exactly what he was up to *and* tell him what she thought of his holiday development.

That settled it. 'Yes, I think I could fit you in, Mr Ritchie,' Lorna heard herself saying as she went in her mind's eye through all the rooms upstairs. None seemed at all suitable for this particular guest, more used as he must surely be to four-star hotels... Still, it had been his choice to come here.

She hadn't forgotten, or forgiven, his gibe about her beloved Land Rover, and she couldn't prevent a coldness creeping into her voice as she remarked, 'It's not very grand here, you know, but I could show you a room before you make up your mind.'

'It's Hobson's choice again, isn't it?' He shrugged. 'As far as I could see, there isn't anywhere else round here where I could stay, even if I wanted to.'

Lorna stiffened. 'You could go into Tobermory if it's a hotel you're after. There are several there that might suit you better, I dare say.'

Martin Ritchie inclined his head just a fraction in brief acknowledgement of the discourtesy of his remark. 'I'm sorry, that must have sounded very rude. As it happens, I can't go anywhere, and I should be very grateful for whatever you can offer me, I assure you.'

His face lit up then with a smile of unexpected charm and brilliance that transformed the saturnine lines of his face and made something coil into a knot deep in the pit of Lorna's stomach.

She fought to control an unevenness in her breath and clenched her hands deep in the safety of her pockets. Damn the man! If he thought he could win her over by the occasional smile, he had another think coming, and Lorna was on the point of telling him she was full up after all before the common sense of sheer economic need prevailed. Business was business, after all.

'If you'd like to follow me, then,' she invited him stiffly, swallowing her pride and instinctive dislike, 'I'll show you to your room. Do you have luggage—a bag?'

'I did bring some things up on the assumption I'd be staying.' Martin Ritchie turned to fetch his case from where he'd left it just outside the front door.

'So your car's still at Archie's, is it?'

Martin Ritchie looked at her darkly with no hint of a smile now on the set lines of his face.

'It'll be there for a couple of days at least,' he said shortly. 'As I said, that's why I'm here needing accommodation.'

'Something serious?' Lorna enquired anxiously, thinking of her precious no-claims bonus.

Her guest shook his head impatiently, hefting his bag from one hand to the other. 'Not very—just inconvenient. Look, could we go up, do you think? This is getting rather heavy.'

Lorna led the way up the stairs, conscious of Martin Ritchie's appraising eyes at her back, no doubt examining everything, including her own rear view—not that she had anything to be ashamed of there, she thought with a little toss of her head. Her energetic lifestyle hardly encouraged the build-up of any flab.

But as they went along the passage to her nicest and most recently refurbished room, Lorna, seeing the house through this stranger's eyes, became uncomfortably aware of the shabbiness of her home. She tried to ignore the threadbare carpet and the faded old-fashioned wallpaper, telling herself that homeliness and warmth were what mattered, and it was all spotless: she prided herself on that. Even so, she thought wistfully, pushing open the bedroom door, new carpeting and a thorough programme of decoration wouldn't come amiss.

This room, at least, was bright and cheerful with its white, freshly painted walls and pretty curtains matching the duvet cover, and the view over the paddocks to the blue haze of distant hills made up for any shortcomings, in Lorna's opinion.

'What do you think?' she asked tentatively. 'Will this suit you? I'm afraid we're not exactly up to Hilton standards here, but the bed is comfortable and you've got a washbasin, and there's a shower next door.'

Martin Ritchie put down his bag, easing his shoulders as he relieved them of their heavy burden, and crossed the floor to stare briefly out of the window.

Then he turned to give Lorna another glimpse of that devastating smile that wrought such havoc with her pulse rate, making her forget, temporarily, the quite different effect he had had on her at the beginning of the day.

'It'll suit me very well—thank you very much, Miss Morrison.'

'And you'll be here one night... two?'

Martin Ritchie's mouth narrowed into more grim lines. 'That depends on how long it'll take your worthy garage mechanic to get the part for my car. He says he'll have to get it flown in from Glasgow, but whether he's capable of fitting it once he's got it is anybody's guess,' he added with a sarcastic flick of his eyebrows.

Lorna flushed with annoyance. 'I've already told you, Archie McIntyre is the best mechanic on the island,' she returned hotly. 'And if he says he can fix it, he will. He may not have the smartest premises you've ever seen, but he can mend anything from a tractor to a Rolls!' she ended defiantly, unsure whether Archie had seen many Rolls-Royces, but she wasn't going to have one of her oldest friends patronised by Mr Martin Ritchie with his Mercedes!

He flung up his hands as though to ward off a blow. *'Touché,'* he said softly with an appreciative gleam in his blue eyes. 'I'm sorry, I've evidently touched a raw spot. I'll give your Mr McIntyre the benefit of any doubts I may have—at least till he gets the car back on the road.'

'Which I'm sure he will, as soon as he gets the part,' Lorna said loyally. 'Now, have you everything you need? Soap, towels...?' She ran her eye round the room and nodded to herself. All seemed to be in order. 'I'll leave you to settle in, then, Mr Ritchie. I'll be downstairs in a short while if there's anything you want or need to know.'

She forced a tight smile, then shut the door firmly behind her before hurrying along to her own room to wash and change.

She stared at her reflection in the mirror. Had she done the right thing, she wondered, by giving Martin Ritchie a room, or should she have sent him packing?

Money wasn't everything, as she'd not hesitated to tell Iain, and by letting him stay hadn't she acted against those very principles she'd been arguing that morning, even if it would give her the chance to find out what he was really up to?

She sighed and ran her hands wearily over her face. Why did life have to be so complicated?

Lorna hadn't been downstairs for long before she heard Jane's car drive up.

'Guess what?' she burst out almost before Jane had got through the back door. 'Guess who's staying the night? That phone call you took, remember?'

'I can't imagine. The Queen? The American president? Mickey Mouse?'

'Ha, ha, very funny.' Lorna pulled a face. 'No—the man I was telling you about, Martin Ritchie. You know, the developer!'

'And you let him in? Really, Lorna! After all you said about him? I wouldn't have thought you'd have let him darken your door.' Jane sat down at the table and shook her head sadly. 'What people will do for money... Ouch!'

Lorna had reached out and pulled her hair. 'Money doesn't come into it—well, not much,' she admitted reluctantly, 'but I thought if he was here, where I could keep an eye on him, I could find out what he really is up to. And put him straight about one or two things. Like how welcome his horrible holiday village would be to some of us,' she ended grimly before swinging round, wide-eyed, at the sound of a step outside in the hall.

Judging from Martin Ritchie's expression she didn't think he'd heard her last remark as he looked from one girl to the other with a pleasant smile.

'This is Mr Ritchie, Jane, Mr Martin Ritchie whom I met this morning,' Lorna said demurely. 'Mr Ritchie, this is my good friend and partner Mrs Jane Baxter.'

Martin Ritchie's smile broadened as he took Jane's outstretched hand, and Lorna was amused to see her friend's brown eyes widen in an instinctive response to the man's undoubted charm similar to her own.

He'd changed from his smart grey flannel suit into an equally smart but casual pair of dark trousers topped by a blue shirt beneath a navy cashmere sweater which set off his dark colouring and accentuated the brighter blue of his eyes. The expensive well-cut clothes made Lorna realise all over again just how tall and good-looking he was, this stranger who had come so unexpectedly into her life.

She looked away quickly, fearing that that sharp gaze might penetrate only too easily into her unsettling thoughts.

'Was there something you needed, Mr Ritchie?' she asked with her back turned towards him as she checked the progress of the potatoes in the oven. 'The room's satisfactory, I hope?'

'Very comfortable, thanks. But there are just a couple of things. One, have you any books I could borrow? I've brought nothing to read and for once in my life I shall actually have time on my hands. And the other thing is, could you tell me where I might get a meal? Are there any restaurants near here?'

Lorna and Jane looked at one another ruefully, and it was Jane who answered.

'There's nowhere nearby at all, Mr Ritchie. The nearest place, the Bothy, is about—oh, six or seven miles away.'

Martin Ritchie's mouth tightened. 'That does seem rather a long walk—or is there a local taxi I could ring? It really is incredibly inconvenient to be without a car.' He smacked one hand into the other in frustration and Lorna suspected he was regretting ever having set foot in a place where so far he'd met nothing but trouble.

'You could ring Duncan,' she began doubtfully, then broke off as she heard Martin Ritchie give a heavy sigh.

'Don't tell me—he's got to come from the other end of the island.'

'Not quite,' Lorna told him cheerfully, 'but by the time he got here, then drove you to the Bothy, even supposing they have room—it gets very full up during the holiday season, you see,' she explained kindly, 'it would be quite late. And then there's the question of getting back here again...'

She flashed him a mischievous glance, taking a malicious pleasure in his expression of dismay, before, to her complete amazement, she heard a voice—*her* voice—speak words that seemed to utter themselves quite involuntarily.

'If you don't mind a very simple meal—and I do mean simple,' she warned him, 'you'd be more than welcome to join the two of us.'

Jane stared at her open-mouthed, well aware that Lorna never, not even for her favourite and most regular visitors, offered an evening meal to her guests. Her evenings were sacrosanct.

'I just can't begin cooking suppers on top of all the other things I have to do,' she'd explained to Jane when they had set up the craft shop together. 'What with this, and the bed and breakfast and pony trekking . . . I must have some time to myself.'

She met Jane's eye now and gave a little shrug, all too aware of what her friend was thinking, and quite unable to explain this impulsive invitation, even to herself.

In fact, she couldn't imagine what had come over her. It was only a short time ago that she had been desperately trying to find a good reason for refusing this man bed and breakfast, and now here she was offering him a meal! This was Highland hospitality run riot, but it was too late to change her mind now.

She watched Martin Ritchie's face brighten with a glimpse of his charming smile.

'That is a very kind offer, Miss Morrison, especially as I can see you were about to have a private meal together. Perhaps I could have mine somewhere else, in another room, rather than impose myself on you?'

Lorna shook her head decisively, making her long plait swing round her head. She caught it and thrust it back over her shoulder.

'We wouldn't hear of it, would we, Jane? I can't leave a guest to go hungry.' She smiled at Martin Ritchie. 'While I'm laying the table, you can be choosing something to read. There are lots of books there, all sorts; some of my father's, and mine, and some left behind by visitors. You should find something to suit you.'

'Lorna, what possessed you?' Jane burst out as Lorna came back into the kitchen after showing Martin Ritchie to the lounge. 'You never feed your guests—you said it was your golden rule! So why this one? No, don't tell me,' she added with a laugh, watching her friend closely. 'You've fallen for those blue eyes and that devastating smile—and I can't say I blame you! I saw you blush!'

'I trust that's meant to be a joke,' Lorna said coldly. 'I'm just doing what anyone would do, as well as lulling him into a false sense of security before I launch my attack on him and all his works.'

'So why all this, for heaven's sake?' Jane persisted, watching with increasing astonishment as Lorna rummaged in the back of a cupboard for a box of coloured candles and matching napkins. 'Are we going to have the best silver, too?'

Lorna shot her a warning look. 'Don't push it, Jane Baxter. There's no reason why we shouldn't make the most of the excuse to have a bit of a party, even if we are only having cold chicken and baked potatoes. And beans, of course.'

Jane wisely held her peace. If Lorna wanted to go to all this trouble for a man she neither knew nor liked, it was none of her business, interesting though it was...

'There,' Lorna said with satisfaction a short time later. 'I think that looks very nice, don't you? I don't imagine Martin Ritchie will feel he's missing out too much on the finer things of life.'

Jane cast an approving eye over the crisp white tablecloth, the yellow candles and napkins, and, in pride of place, a venerable bottle of claret, glowing red against the candle-flames.

'I think you've done him—all of us—proud, and he should be extremely impressed, as well as grateful.'

'Well, I'd better go and see, then, hadn't I?'

After a quick glance at her reflection in the hall mirror to smooth her hair into place, Lorna made her way to the lounge to fetch her guest. Something about the way he was sitting, lost in a book and clearly quite at home in the big armchair that had been her father's, caught at her throat and she gave a dry little cough, making Martin Ritchie look up, smiling.

'Supper's ready, Mr Ritchie, if you'd like to come through.'

He unwound his limbs with a careless grace, marking the place in his book with a slip of paper from his trouser pocket. 'Martin, please...'

Lorna was annoyed to feel her cheeks grow warm. 'And I'm Lorna.'

Martin crossed the room with a few long strides, reaching out to hold the door for her, and as he did so his arm brushed against hers, setting up again that disturbing tingle she'd felt earlier when he'd taken her hand.

What was happening? Lorna thought in alarm. This was something she certainly hadn't bargained for—that he would be able to work his undoubted charm on her and make her forget all her earlier antipathy towards him, how he'd been so rude... She mustn't trust him an inch, she reminded herself severely. Just remember why he was here on the island—what he'd come to do.

Martin's face lit up when they reached the kitchen. 'My goodness!' he exclaimed. 'I thought you said it was only to be a simple meal—or do you always eat like this?' His eye fell on the bottle of wine. 'And that claret,' he added in a tone of deep respect, 'looks very far from ordinary.'

'My father had quite a good cellar,' Lorna explained, 'and as I don't get many opportunities to sample it, I thought we might give ourselves a treat this evening. It'll be all right, won't it? I know it hasn't been open very long, but unless you want to postpone the meal...?'

Martin pulled a rueful face. 'I am actually quite hungry—it's been a pretty long day, one way and the other.'

'That settles it, then,' Lorna proclaimed firmly. 'Would you mind pouring the wine, then, Martin, while I serve the chicken?' Lorna looked at him sideways from beneath her thick golden lashes. 'I hope you see now that we're not quite so unsophisticated as you thought we were this morning. I know your opinion of our road system, but some of us are capable of appreciating the finer things of life.'

'So I see,' Martin murmured, serving the wine with the care due to its age. 'I shall do my best to remember it, I promise.'

Jane was astonished at this lively interchange. She didn't know when, if ever, she had seen Lorna so animated. Iain had certainly never inspired such vivacity in her friend, whose green eyes positively sparkled as she looked at Martin across the table.

As for Lorna herself, as the evening wore on she found it increasingly hard to remember she wasn't supposed to *like* this man who was engaging them all in a lively conversation ranging from the history of the Highlands to books and the theatre, even politics.

And what of her earlier suspicions about his reasons for being here at all? Wasn't it about time she tried to find out?

She looked at him covertly as he turned once again to speak to Jane. Could she have been mistaken about him, after all? Could this interesting and undoubtedly charming man really be the evil developer she had assumed him to be, only intent on the destruction of her beloved island? Maybe not...and yet he hadn't been quite so charming that morning, had he? He'd been downright rude then, if not actually offensive. But supposing...

Martin looked up just at that moment and met her pensive stare with a smile.

'Tell me something, Martin,' Lorna put in quickly before she could change her mind. 'You said you were here on business, but you haven't mentioned your work all evening. What do you actually do—for a living, that is? Or is it a secret?'

She watched Martin carefully as one eyebrow went up.

'Nothing very exciting, and it's certainly no secret. I'm in the travel business, that's all. I'd never been to Mull and thought I'd have a look round while I was over on the West coast. Satisfied, Miss Morrison?'

Lorna's lips tightened. Travel meant holidays, and holidays were spent—by some people—at the kind of development Iain's customers had been so excited about. She wasn't convinced, not yet.

'You're not in the property business, then? You're not here to build a holiday camp?'

There was no mistaking the surprise on Martin's face.

'A holiday camp? Good grief, Lorna! Whatever gave you that idea?'

Lorna beamed with relief at his tacit denial of her question. 'Just a rumour going round. That's OK, then. Come on, finish up the wine, and I'll put the coffee on.'

Martin opened his mouth to comment on this peculiar interrogation, then thought better of it, draining the last of his hostess's wine instead as Lorna guided the conversation back to less controversial topics.

At last Jane looked at her watch. 'Goodness, is that the time? I must be off.' She pushed back her chair and got to her feet. 'Come on, Lorna, let me give you a hand clearing up, then I must be on my way.'

'Out of the question,' Martin said firmly. 'That's my job, and the least I can do under the circumstances—no argument.'

Jane looked helplessly from Martin to Lorna and back again. 'It doesn't seem right, but if you're sure...?'

Martin nodded. 'Quite sure. I'm a dab hand at drying, and it won't take us any time at all. I'll see you again, I hope?'

'Tomorrow, I expect,' Jane smiled, 'and thanks a lot, Lorna. It's been a lovely evening.'

'She's nice, Jane, isn't she?' Martin commented a few minutes later as he went to stand over by the sink. 'Is she an islander like you, or has she come over from the mainland?'

While they cleared away the dishes and Lorna stowed them in the dishwasher—one of the few modern aids she'd splashed out on when she had begun her bed and breakfast venture, and hardly a luxury in the circumstances, she'd decided—she told Martin how Jane had been left high and dry by the man she'd married while still at university.

'That's where we met,' Lorna explained, 'and although we weren't particularly close friends then, I don't know what I'd do without her now.'

'You run the craft shop together, do you?' Martin leant back against the table and folded his arms.

Lorna nodded. 'Jane discovered quite by chance that she has a real gift for making jewellery—silver work, mostly—and when we met at a students' reunion she asked me whether I knew anywhere on the island that would be interested in selling her things. Then one thing led to another, and she decided to come and live here. She lives in a cottage in the village and she divides her time between her studio and the shop. It works quite well.'

'You work very hard, don't you, the two of you?' Martin observed as he watched Lorna tidy away the last of the dishes and begin to lay the table again ready for the morning. 'Do you ever take any time off?'

'Not often,' Lorna replied cheerfully. 'Just a day or two in the winter to go and see my mother in Edinburgh. It's difficult, you see, if you keep animals. They always need looking after.'

'And what about you, Miss Morrison? Who looks after you?' A different note sounded in the deep voice, catching Lorna unawares, and something she read in the blue eyes fixed on her face made her turn quickly to realign a knife more precisely on the table. Still fiddling with it, she managed a light laugh.

'Oh, I don't need looking after. We come tough up here, Mr Ritchie. I manage just fine on my own.'

'I can see that,' Martin agreed as he looked round the big kitchen, spotless and shipshape. 'But doesn't it get lonely sometimes, here all by yourself?'

Lorna grinned. 'I hardly ever am by myself, what with the bed and breakfast visitors, the people who come to ride my ponies, the customers in the shop... In fact, sometimes I just long for some time on my own. And in any case, this is a very close-knit community and as I've lived here all my life I have a lot of very good friends. There's always company if I need it.'

'"Very good"?' Martin repeated softly with a meaningful glance at her left hand. 'You're not married, but are you spoken for, perhaps?'

'Spoken for?' Lorna did her best to ignore the note of warmth that had crept into Martin's voice, sending a shiver wriggling down her spine. 'That would be telling, wouldn't it?'

The words slipped out before she could stop them, and it was too late now to recall them and tell him about Iain and their unspoken understanding. Not that there was any reason why she should have told him—it was strictly a private matter—but neither was there any reason why she *shouldn't* have told him.

'So you're not?' Martin was obviously not going to let her get away lightly.

'Not what?' Innocently she raised her eyes to Martin's, unable to suppress a little *frisson* in her heart as she caught the humorous glint in their sea-blue depths.

'Going to tell me?'

'There's nothing to tell,' she replied as evenly as she could, and that was no lie, at least.

'So there's no great hulking Highlander lurking out there with a claymore, about to whisk you off to his castle—or even a croft?' Martin persisted.

'Certainly not.'

She saw Martin's mouth twitch at her fierce denial and his lips curved into a smile as she snatched up a cloth to rub away at some imaginary mark on the stove, but he said nothing more and when Lorna finally turned round he was standing by the window, staring out at the twilit garden.

The dangerous corner seemed to have been avoided, and Lorna took advantage of his silence to change the subject to safer and more mundane matters.

'I shall have to be up early tomorrow—I have a ride to take out after breakfast—so I think I'll turn in now, but please, do stay downstairs as long as you like and make yourself at home. There's some whisky in the dresser there if you'd like a nightcap.'

For answer Martin suddenly reached out and laid a hand on her arm, sending a thrill shooting along her nerve-ends which she was convinced he must be able to sense as her muscles tensed to his touch.

'Thank you for the meal, Lorna, and for a most enjoyable evening.' The normally severe contours of his face softened as the pressure of his fingers tightened briefly. 'And I'm glad the day hasn't ended as it began. All's well that ends well, I suppose you could say?'

I'd call it more confusing than anything else, Lorna thought as she climbed the stairs to her room. If anyone had told her that morning that she would willingly be offering hospitality to *him*—Martin Ritchie, of all people—she'd never have believed them. And no ordinary hospitality, either, but an invitation to supper and a bottle of her father's best claret!

Lorna sat on the edge of her bed and began to unplait her hair, brushing it with long, rhythmic strokes until it covered her shoulders in a heavy golden curtain.

At least she was more or less certain now that Martin had nothing to do with the holiday scheme. There was no reason she could think of why he shouldn't have been telling the truth, and that look of surprise when she'd suggested he might be in the property business couldn't have been feigned.

If anyone had been secretive, it had been her, she realised with a jolt of conscience. Why she hadn't told him she was as good as 'spoken for', as he had put it, she couldn't imagine, unless...

That was plain ridiculous. She'd only known Martin Ritchie a day, and for half of that she'd believed him to be the most odious man she had ever met. There was no question that she could be seriously attracted to him, none at all. He just wasn't her type.

CHAPTER THREE

THERE was neither sight nor sound of her visitor when Lorna went downstairs early the following morning to snatch a hasty cup of tea before going to fetch the ponies in from the paddock. Fiona, her young helper from the village, would be here later to help her get them ready for the morning's ride, but bringing her old friends in to the stable-yard and giving them their morning feed was a job she liked to do herself, especially on a morning as beautiful as this, mild and clear with the promise of a lovely day to come.

She hummed happily to herself as she went back into the kitchen.

'Good morning, Lorna.'

She stopped in the doorway, surprised to find Martin already up and sitting at her kitchen table, looking perfectly at home with a copy of the last week's edition of the local paper spread out before him. Her coffee percolator was bubbling away and a smell of freshly made toast filled the air, reminding her she hadn't yet had anything to eat and was very hungry.

'Oh . . . good morning.' She smiled cheerfully at him, her heart giving a little jump as she registered all over again just how good-looking he was, so tall and dark with those startlingly blue eyes—eyes now fixed consideringly on her face.

'I'm sorry if I've taken liberties, but when I came down there wasn't any sign of life, so I took matters into my own hands, as you see. Have you had any breakfast?'

He got up and went over to pour them both a cup of coffee and Lorna laughed.

'I see I shall have to knock something off your bill. I don't usually expect my guests to have to serve themselves, let alone make my breakfast as well, but if there is any toast going...?'

They sat companionably either side of the big table and Lorna tucked into her toast and marmalade with a gusto that made Martin raise his eyebrows.

'Have you been up long?' he enquired with a grin. 'You seem to have worked up quite an appetite, if I may say so.'

'It's the open air,' Lorna explained, her mouth full, 'and the unexpected treat of having breakfast made for me. Toast always tastes better if someone else has made it. Thanks... Oh,' she added hastily as she rather belatedly remembered her status as Martin's landlady, 'did you sleep well? I hope the fact you're up so early doesn't mean your bed was uncomfortable?'

'No, not at all. In fact...' Martin tilted his chair back and linked his arms behind his head '...I don't know when I've had a better night's sleep. It's so calm and peaceful here—I'd forgotten what I've been missing, cooped up in the city. The air's so fresh you can almost taste it, can't you? No traffic, no pollution—marvellous!'

'That's good,' Lorna said, pleased, and her spirits lifted on a surge of relief as any last doubts she might have had about Martin's work evaporated with his words. 'I mentioned last night, didn't I, that there's a rumour that some company from the mainland wants to build a holiday village or leisure complex—I don't know exactly what, but something like that, anyway—here on the island, probably on the north coast in one of the quietest and most beautiful parts?'

Martin sat up and looked at her sharply. 'Yes, I remember. In fact, I was going to ask you about that. Thanks for reminding me.' He frowned and tapped the end of his knife against the table. 'Is it still only a rumour, do you know, or is there more to it than that? Were you told whether it had got to the planning stage yet?'

Lorna stared at him in surprise and with some sudden misgivings. 'I don't know,' she said slowly. 'I only heard about it yesterday. It came as quite a shock, actually.'

Again she searched his expression for a clue to what he was thinking, but he was giving nothing away as he sat digesting the information she'd just given him.

'A holiday village, they said? I wonder...? Still, I dare say it's early days yet, and maybe nothing will come of it. I shouldn't worry too much.'

'I'm not worried, just angry,' Lorna burst out, unable to keep her feelings to herself any longer. 'Especially at the people—friends of mine, some of them—who are in favour of the development.' She cracked down her cup with a ferocity that made Martin's eyes refocus in some surprise on her face. 'They say it'd bring business and jobs to the island, but I told them we can do without that sort of business, thank you very much.'

'But they'd be right, wouldn't they?' Martin remarked reasonably, then grinned. 'And someone would have to do something about the roads, too, which certainly wouldn't be a bad thing!'

'And have everybody driving like maniacs?' Lorna shot at him, not appreciating the joke. 'No, thank you.'

She pushed back her chair roughly and swept up her plate and cup to march over to the sink, disappointed at Martin's reaction which had been ambiguous to say the least, and unsettling too, just when she'd thought she could lay her suspicions finally to rest. The only way she could find out what she wanted to know was to ask him straight out.

She took a deep breath.

'Martin...?' But even as she spoke she decided against a direct confrontation. This was neither the time nor the place for a full-scale argument, for she knew only too well that she would not be able to control her tongue if her earlier suspicions proved after all to be correct.

She turned to face him to find him looking at her expectantly.

'Yes?'

She thought quickly for something to say to change the subject. 'I suppose breaking down yesterday has prevented you getting on with whatever business you came here to do?' she ventured brightly. 'Exploring the island, or whatever. Have you any plans for today?'

Martin's lips compressed with irritation.

'Since you ask, yes, it is most inconvenient to be without any transport. It's going to put back my schedule quite considerably, being stuck here.' He too got up and began to pace the floor impatiently. 'I suppose your Archie McIntyre wouldn't have anything I could hire, then at least I could get round the place?'

Lorna pursed her lips. 'You could try, I suppose, but I shouldn't have thought so. Where d'you want to go?'

Martin shrugged. 'I can't say without my maps, and I've left those in the car. It's so frustrating!' He snapped one fist into the other and resumed pacing once more. 'If there's one thing I can't stand, it's waste, especially waste of time!'

'Maps are no problem,' Lorna told him. 'I've got plenty, but transport...I don't know what to suggest.'

She glanced out of the window at the blue sky. 'As you are "stuck here", as you put it, and more or less at a loose end, why don't you make the most of it and go for a good walk? I could tell you where to go. It's going to be a lovely day,' she added temptingly.

'I told you, I don't like wasting time, and ambling round the countryside on my own would be just that, so far as I'm concerned. No, I'll stay here. I've plenty of paperwork to catch up on, and phone calls to make. I ought at least to tell the office where I am.'

He caught sight of Lorna's wide-eyed expression of mild outrage and a slight smile curved his mouth. 'I should have asked you if that would be convenient, I suppose. You did say you would be out on a ride, so I won't be in anybody's way, will I?'

It was a statement rather than a question and did nothing to quell the surge of resentment Lorna felt at the way he seemed to take her hospitality for granted.

'Bed and breakfast guests are expected to vacate their rooms by ten o'clock,' she pointed out tartly. 'I *am* out all morning, as it happens, but I don't make a habit of leaving my house open for all and sundry to come and go. I wouldn't know what strangers might come and make themselves free of it,' she added with a meaningful glint in her eye.

Martin's eyebrows rose lazily. 'But I'm not, am I?'

'Not what?'

'A stranger—or a bed and breakfast guest. You invited me for a meal, which puts me in a different category altogether.' The ironic set of his features relaxed suddenly into that devastating smile so effective against all her defences, and in spite of all her best efforts to harden her heart to his almost hypnotic charm she heard herself capitulate feebly.

'No,' she sighed. 'You won't be in anyone's way, and I suppose you have nowhere else to go, have you?'

'Unless there's an empty stable I could sit in?'

Lorna caught at her thick plait, edgily twining the end round her fingers. 'That's ridiculous, and of course there's no question of that. In any case, I have no time to argue. My helper will be here by now and I, too, have work to get on with.' She pulled the door open and stood glaring back at him. 'You'd better stay here, I suppose,' she told him, ungracious in defeat, 'and please, do make yourself quite at home!'

Drat the man, she thought, not for the first time. It had been against her better judgement that she had put him up at all, and then, before she knew it, she had been offering him a meal...and now here he was settling down in her home for the whole day. If she wasn't careful, he'd become a permanent fixture, constantly getting his own way by a combination of charm and a neat line in sarcasm.

But now there were other matters that needed her attention and, even though Mr Martin Ritchie was still occupying her house, she must make sure she put him from her thoughts, and a good, long ride would help her do just that.

The island was looking at its very best that morning, the sunlit sweeps of heather and bracken stretching away to the misty peak of Ben More on one side and towards the sea on the other, and the air was clear enough as the riders approached the coast to give a rare glimpse of the Cuillin Hills on the Isle of Skye.

So when someone suggested that they extend the ride into the afternoon, Lorna willingly agreed, and it wasn't until quite late that they all clattered into the stable-yard at Glenmore; by the time that Lorna and Fiona had unsaddled, fed and groomed the ponies Lorna at least was feeling hot, tired and very hungry.

'I don't know about you,' she groaned when they had finally finished all the chores, 'but I'm *starving*! Come on, I'll make us some sandwiches. It won't take a minute.'

'Thanks, Lorna,' Fiona said, 'but if it's all the same to you I'll be away home and get a bite there. I promised Mum I'd be there when the twins get back from school—she's away to see my Auntie Nora.'

'OK, then,' Lorna returned cheerfully, 'if you're sure. Thanks for staying on—see you tomorrow.'

She crossed the yard, passing Jane's car parked by the wall of the house. She'd go into the shop to see her in a while, but first she must have a wash and get something to eat.

Then she remembered. Martin. Would he still be there? A mingled sense of unease and anticipation quivered through her as her hand hesitated over the doorknob to move instinctively to smooth back the tendrils of hair sticking to her hot face.

Slowly she pushed open the door, but almost to her relief there was no sign of him, only his papers stacked tidily on the table with his briefcase. He must have changed his mind and gone out after all.

She rinsed her hands under the tap, cut some bread, and was just crossing to the fridge to see what she could find to make into a sandwich when her eye was caught by the heading on the topmost sheet of paper beside Martin's briefcase.

'Enterprise Tours', she read slowly and in disbelief, picking it up to study it more closely. '"Enterprise Tours",' she repeated out loud—no, there was no mistake. '"Park Street, Glasgow. Directors, C. Langdon, W.P. MacPharlane... M.D. Ritchie..."'

There it was in black and white, the indisputable evidence she had been searching for, dancing now before her eyes as the paper shook in her fingers.

Lorna sat down heavily and dropped her hand on to the table, running her eyes down the page yet hardly taking in what she was reading in Martin's unfamiliar handwriting. He seemed to have been making notes, itemising various landmarks and beauty spots on the island with comments as to their suitability for some unspecified but only too obvious purpose connected with the holiday trade.

'Parking facilities non-existent,' she read against one entry. 'Roads primitive, but scenery spectacular.'

So she had been right, after all, and all her suspicions justified. A slow fuse began to smoulder in Lorna's brain, making her forget all about her hunger and earlier fatigue.

'Martin Ritchie, director,' she read again. And here he was trying to find a site for his loathsome holiday camp, and the reason why he had pricked up his ears when she'd told him about the rumour was because he wanted it kept secret, at least until the details were all sorted out and the planning application before the authorities.

If only she had known... She'd never, not in a million years, have let him even cross the threshold, let alone have invited him to supper, nor, she fumed inwardly, seeing the empty bottle still on the draining-board, opened one of her father's special clarets.

In her mind's eye the landscape she and her party had marvelled at only an hour or two ago unfolded again: the calm beauty of the moors and woods, the tranquillity of the lochs beneath the eggshell sky and above all the pervading quiet—all this was under threat from this...this plausible and deceitful vandal and his 'Enterprise Tours'!

Thank goodness Jane was here! She must go and tell her at once... And then, Lorna thought grimly, her first priority would be to find Martin Ritchie and tell him a few home truths before making it quite clear that he was no longer welcome in her home. He'd have to pack up his things and go immediately, she didn't care how or where...

She almost ran out of the house and round the corner to the shop.

'Jane!' Lorna stopped, the words frozen on her lips as she stood unnoticed in the doorway, watching Jane's uplifted face alight with laughter at some remark made by her companion.

Some spark Lorna refused to recognise as jealousy fuelled her already smouldering temper into a blaze of anger as her eyes moved to the tall, elegant figure leaning nonchalantly against the wall, his back turned to her.

For a while she remained unnoticed by the two so involved in their conversation, laughing and joking as though they were old friends, until at last Jane's attention was caught by the figure blocking out the sunlight.

'Lorna! Come on in—you're late, aren't you? Was it a good ride?'

Lorna muttered something non-committal, but kept her eyes fixed on Martin as she crossed the floor to thrust the incriminating document towards him.

'Is this yours?'

Martin straightened up slowly, the smile fading from his face. 'You know very well it is. Do you make a habit of reading other people's papers, Miss Morrison?'

The words were spoken lightly enough, but there was no mistaking the danger signals glinting in the deep blue eyes.

'Only when they affect me or my home.'

Jane looked from one to the other with mounting astonishment. 'What...?'

Lorna waved a dismissive hand. 'Just wait. I'll explain in a minute. This is your company, I presume?' she asked, addressing Martin again. '"Enterprise Tours"?'

Martin reached out a long arm and took the paper from Lorna's hand. 'Yes, it is, though I fail to see what business it is of yours. As for there being any connection with your home, it is the last——'

'Not Glenmore; the whole island, I meant,' Lorna interrupted him fiercely. She swung round to Jane. 'I knew all along he was hiding something, and I was right. He lied to us last night when he said he had nothing to do with the holiday camp. He's actually a director of this tour company——' she gestured towards the paper now in Martin's hand '—and he's only here to sus out the place, there's no doubt at all about that. You only have to read what he's got written down there. He's the one who's going to ruin the island!'

Martin took a step nearer to her. 'I have no idea what you're talking about,' he said with icy coldness, 'and I suggest you calm down before you say something you'll regret.'

'Don't you patronise me!' stormed Lorna. 'And I have nothing whatever to regret. It's you who'll regret ever having set foot on our island when you see the fight you're going to have on your hands. Not everyone thinks money and profits are the most important things in life, you know. Some of us actually enjoy the peace and quiet of what you think is just a primitive backwater, and you may find it hard to believe, but people do still come here for their holidays just because it is so peaceful—and to escape all those so-called amenities you want to inflict on us!'

Martin had made no attempt to interrupt her, and while she had been talking had resumed his position against the wall, thrusting his hands deep into his pockets and jingling his change, an action calculated to infuriate her still further.

He looked down now into her angry face with a mocking smile on his lips.

'Quite a speech,' he said with ironic admiration, 'but if you have finished, I think there's something you ought to know.'

'There's nothing you can tell me that I want to hear,' Lorna retorted, 'but I know enough to realise I made a big mistake letting you stay here. I should be grateful, Mr Ritchie, if you would leave as soon as you can. I'll make out your account and have it ready by the time you've packed.'

She swung round to march out of the shop but felt her arm seized in a grip of iron which only tightened as she struggled to pull free.

'Let me go!' she blazed. 'Or I'll——'

'Or you'll do what?' Martin asked lightly, his deep voice tinged with amusement. 'I don't think you'll find you can do very much, not until I choose to let you.'

Their eyes met in an unspoken challenge of wills but Lorna held his gaze, determined not to give in an inch. She was in the right, after all.

'You deceived me,' she accused him. 'When I told you about the development this morning you let me think you had nothing to do with it.' She gave a bitter laugh. 'It was a good act you put on, and you fooled me properly, pretending not to know anything about it, when all the time——'

'I should be careful, Miss Morrison, accusing people of deception without any foundation. It could land you in a deal of trouble. There is such a thing as the law of slander, you know, and I have a witness.'

They both looked round, but Jane had slipped quietly away leaving the two of them alone to fight it out.

'Wise woman, Jane,' Martin observed drily. His grip on Lorna's arm hardened and he pulled her close so that she was forced to look straight up into his face. 'I have no need to justify myself in any way, but I should just like to point out that my company has no interest in holiday camps, villages, developments or complexes of any kind, although,' he went on thoughtfully, 'even if it were, it's hardly a crime, is it, to create something which would give a lot of pleasure to a great many people and bring some badly needed prosperity to the community into the bargain?'

Lorna chose to ignore this and concentrated her attack on the first part of his statement. 'Why should I believe you when I saw with my own eyes what you'd written? "Check out holiday development". It's there, isn't it, in your handwriting? You can't deny it.'

'I've no intention of denying it.' Martin's lean face darkened as he towered over her, not relinquishing his hold of her arm, and Lorna found herself having to suppress a tiny tremor, not of fear exactly, but certainly of apprehension. He had a temper, this man, hot enough to match her own, and he held her prisoner...

'I don't need to deny or admit anything to you, Miss Morrison,' he rasped, 'and I think this has gone quite far enough. What I've told you in all good faith you can choose whether to believe or not—that is your affair—but I am not accustomed to having my word doubted.'

He dropped her arm then and Lorna stepped quickly back, rubbing her arm where he had bruised it in his hard fingers.

For the briefest instant Martin's face softened as he took in the red weals on her skin, but the moment passed, leaving his features as grimly set as before.

'There is one thing we agree about, at least,' he said coldly. 'I shall be leaving as soon as I've packed, so if you'll make up the bill...?' He strode off to the door where he paused. 'Oh, and add the cost of a couple of phone calls. I'll be needing a taxi to take me to a hotel somewhere, wherever it has to come from.'

Lorna subsided on to a chair, feeling furious and at the same time somehow deflated, but before she could decide what her next move should be a face peered round the door leading to the stockroom, eyes wide in mock trepidation.

'Is it safe to come in?' Jane asked in a stage whisper. 'Or is the shop about to explode from spontaneous combustion?'

'Come in,' Lorna said wearily. 'Martin's left—in fact, he's leaving altogether, for good.'

'Oh, Lorna.' Jane came across and rested her hand on her friend's shoulder with an exasperated but affectionate smile. 'It's not for me to say, but——'

'—but you're going to, and I know what. You think I've gone over the top, but——'

'No, listen to me,' Jane said more firmly. 'Martin really hasn't anything at all to do with your development.'

'It's not *my* development!'

'OK, OK—don't fly off the handle again! Just let me finish! What I was going to say was that I know for a fact his company is in quite another line of business, only you never let either of us get a word in to explain.'

'So what does he do?' Lorna's voice was bleak.

'He runs a very high-class tour company—trips laid on for wives of visiting VIPs, conference delegates, the rich and discerning, you know the sort of people. They take them round historical sites, beauty spots, nature reserves and so on, all in very superior coaches, staying at the best hotels...'

There was a long pause while Lorna tried to come to terms with this information. Coaches needed wide roads, didn't they? Roads where you didn't run into sheep, or angry girls in Land Rovers—and places to park...?

'Oh, dear,' she said weakly, feeling her cheeks redden. 'I begin to see——'

'And,' Jane went on remorselessly, 'Martin actually did come here to "sus out" the island, as you put it, not to plant holiday chalets all over it, but to decide whether and how he could include Mull in his Highlands and Islands itinerary.'

Lorna sighed again more heavily, and her shoulders sagged. 'There's not much to say, is there?'

'Except "sorry"?' Jane suggested.

'If you think——' Lorna began hotly, then caught Jane's eye and bowed her head, struggling with pride and conscience. At last she got up and managed a weak grin at her own expense. 'I've made a bit of a fool of myself, haven't I? And Martin Ritchie's not the sort of man to let me forget it, not that I'd blame him.' She gave a sort of groan. 'The customer's always supposed to be right, isn't he? Maybe I'm not cut out to be a landlady. Shall I throw it all up and go and get a job in Edinburgh—tell Mum she was right all along?'

'Don't be silly—oh, and that reminds me.' Jane fished in her pocket and held out a slip of paper. 'These people—the Collinses—rang up to book a bed for the night. I didn't think you were full, so I said it was all right.'

Lorna took the paper with a sigh. 'Yes, it is; apart from Martin there's no one staying, and if I don't go and sort things out I'll be losing him as well, won't I? I'd better go and get it over with. Wish me luck.'

There was no sign of Martin or of his papers in the kitchen, only her discarded slices of bread on the table. She stared at them unenthusiastically, her appetite gone, and made her reluctant way upstairs to try to repair the damage she had done.

Martin's bedroom door was ajar and she could see him moving round inside the room, apparently collecting up his belongings before stowing them away in his bag. It must be now or never.

Timidly she knocked on the door.

'Yes, come in!' came the brusque reply, then, as Lorna pushed the door open, Martin went on without even looking round, 'Have you brought the bill?'

'I haven't made it out yet,' Lorna answered in a low voice. 'I'll do it in a minute, if you still want to leave, but first there's something I have to say.'

She couldn't see his face as he bent over the bed, folding a shirt with immaculate precision, and somewhere, deep in the pit of her stomach, Lorna felt the familiar flutter as she took in the almost graceful curve of his back beneath the soft sweater and the taut muscles of his thighs braced against the edge of the mattress.

'Well?' The harsh voice brought Lorna back to earth.

'All I wanted to say was that I'm sorry—very sorry,' she said quickly, wanting to get the ordeal over. 'I realise now that I should never have sounded off as I did just now. I put two and two together and made about twenty-four,' she added ruefully before going on more slowly, 'You see, I'd only just heard about the development when I met you on the road yesterday, and, well, you know the rest.'

There was a slight pause while Martin picked up a sweater to fold it with meticulous care. 'Do you always leap to such impulsive conclusions?' he asked lightly. 'If so, it can't do much for your blood-pressure.'

Lorna let her spirits rise a fraction at the new tone in his voice. 'I think I probably do, especially when I care a lot about something,' she admitted. 'I know I ought to look before I leap, but I never seem to remember until it's too late.'

'I see.' Martin turned now to face her, and Lorna's heart fell again as she saw his stony expression. 'Even so, laudable though your intentions may have been on this occasion, it never does any harm to get your facts right before coming in with all guns blazing.'

'I know,' Lorna acknowledged helplessly. 'But I have admitted I was wrong, and you still haven't said whether you accept my apology. What more do you want me to do? Grovel?'

Her green eyes flashed, mirroring an answering gleam in Martin's blue ones.

'That would be a novel experience,' he murmured thoughtfully, his mouth twitching. 'It's a long time since anyone grovelled to me, especially anybody so pretty.'

Lorna flushed. 'I came up to try to put things right, and all you can do is make fun of me. I'm sorry; it was obviously a waste of time for both of us. I'll go and get your bill—and would you like me to ring the taxi? Then you won't have to spend any longer here than absolutely necessary,' she added drily.

Martin straightened up to look directly at her, and to her surprise he had a broad grin on his face. 'Your good resolutions don't last long, do they? If that's not leaping to conclusions, I don't know what is.'

He took a step nearer to stand so close that she was forced to tilt her head back, her pulses quickening in response to the humorous light in his eyes, the almost sensuous curve to his lips. Supposing...? Swiftly she edged back into the doorway, horrified at the direction her thoughts were taking, but Martin didn't appear to notice anything unusual as he went on, 'You never gave me a chance to get a word in, did you? You've simply made assumptions—again! I have actually decided to stay on, if it's convenient, that is?'

He strolled over to the window to stare out at the view, his hands clasped behind his broad back.

'I've taken quite a liking to this room—and the service in this guest-house is actually quite attentive, so long as the landlady isn't too taken up with the bees buzzing round her bonnet,' he added casually.

Lorna felt her cheeks grow pink. 'Of course it's convenient,' she asserted, deciding to ignore the last part of his sentence. 'I just didn't think you would possibly want to stay on here after... you know,' she ended weakly.

'Well, you were wrong again, weren't you?' Martin remarked, not unkindly. 'And I think it's about time we forgot all about our—your—misunderstanding. Seal our truce?'

He held out his hand and Lorna put hers into it, feeling his fingers close, warm and hard, round her own.

'A truce,' she repeated gratefully, 'and thanks.'

'Right, so now that's settled, I wonder whether you would do something for me?' Martin asked briskly, releasing her hand as he moved away to begin the job of replacing his things in the drawers he'd only just emptied.

'Yes, of course,' Lorna replied curiously, slightly bemused at yet another change of mood.

'Could you get hold of this elusive taxi-driver and see if he could pick me up at, say, six-thirty? Then book me a table somewhere suitable for dinner. For two,' he added as though as an afterthought.

'For two,' Lorna echoed bleakly. He and Jane must have been getting on even better than she had suspected that afternoon—until she had interrupted their tête-à-tête with her unfounded accusations. Oh, well, it only served her right.

She suppressed a sigh as she said with forced brightness, 'I'll see what I can do.'

'Thanks, Lorna. And if you could tell me whether you've managed to be successful I'd be very grateful.'

CHAPTER FOUR

LORNA trudged off downstairs again, making a valiant effort to keep her mind on the task in hand without letting it dwell on her disappointment that it wasn't she who would be sharing Martin's table for two, although after her quite unfounded attack on him there was no earthly reason why he should have the slightest desire to spend any longer in her company than was absolutely necessary. In his shoes she'd probably have left on the spot.

She arranged for the taxi to pick Martin up and stood, frowning, weighing the receiver in her hand as she wondered where to book him and Jane in for dinner.

It's nice for Jane to have a treat, she told herself loyally, and Martin would be a charming and attentive host, she was sure, and a generous one, too. It would have to be the Galleon, easily the most expensive restaurant on Mull and probably anywhere in the Hebrides, but the prices were matched by the quality of the cooking.

As she dialled the number she thought fleetingly that it was strange that Jane hadn't mentioned her date with Martin, but then events had rather taken over, and she'd scarcely given her friend any chance to tell her anything, had she?

The Galleon was very busy later in the evening—a party off one of the yachts in the harbour, they said—but if Mr Ritchie and his guest could arrive early, they could find them a table. Well, that would fit in with the taxi, and Lorna knew Jane didn't like being out late, so she felt quite pleased with herself as she climbed wearily upstairs again to find Martin and tell him what she had arranged.

As she passed the bathroom door, Lorna felt a sudden yearning for the wash and meal so long postponed. Once she'd seen Mr and Mrs Collins settled in she promised herself a long soak before settling down for a really relaxing evening with the TV or a book, though of course she could go down to the village and see Iain, and take the opportunity to make up their differences.

Normally she'd have jumped at the chance of spending an evening with her oldest friend... Lorna's thoughts trailed off unenthusiastically, and not simply because of their disagreement. Somehow the prospect just didn't appeal, not today.

Martin's bedroom door was shut now, and Lorna knocked tentatively.

'Martin? I've fixed everything—shall I come back later and tell you what I've done?'

There was a sound from inside, then the door opened and Lorna stopped short, unable to suppress an all too audible gasp at the sight of the semi-naked male figure clad only in a towel wrapped round his hips. Discomfited as much by her own reactions as by this vision of uncompromising masculinity, she dropped her gaze, so didn't see the amusement flicker across Martin's dark features.

'I was on the way to have a shower,' he explained with a twitch of his lips. 'There aren't any other guests around, are there? No one I might shock by my state of undress?'

Was he making fun of her? Lorna wondered as her eyes moved from their ever so casual perusal of the wallpaper to travel up the tall, muscular frame till they reached the more familiar contours of his face to find those quizzical blue eyes waiting for her, glinting at her painfully obvious agitation.

Her pulse raced as she fought to control an almost desperate urge to reach out and touch that smooth skin, to feel the hardness of his strong body pressed to her soft curves.

This was madness. She gulped down a swallow as she made a valiant effort to keep her voice steady, thrusting her hands deep into her pockets.

'No, not yet, though another couple are coming later,' she told him, annoyed to feel her cheeks grow warm under his amused scrutiny.

'The taxi's coming at six-thirty,' she went on, trying her best to sound coolly competent but failing dismally as he remained standing there, just watching her. 'I've booked you and Jane a table at the Galleon in Tobermory. It is rather expensive, I'm afraid, and I hope I did the right thing, but it is very good, and I don't think you'll be disappointed.'

'Disappointed.' Martin repeated the word thoughtfully, and grinned. 'We'll have to see, won't we, Jane and I?'

'It really is good,' Lorna protested. 'As good as anywhere you've got in Glasgow. It's in all the food guides with stars and whatever.'

'I'm sure.' Martin nodded gravely, giving a hitch to his towel, an action which did nothing for Lorna's state of mind. 'So I'd better get a move on, hadn't I? Especially if I'm going to collect Jane first.' Again his eyes glinted mischievously as Lorna backed away to let him get past her, his bare arm almost, but not quite, touching her.

'And what will you do this evening?' he asked her over his shoulder as he walked along the passage.

Lorna let her eyes slide longingly over the bare back, yearning again to feel the muscles tense to her caress, then bringing herself up short. What was she thinking of?

'Me? Oh, not much,' she replied with a light laugh. 'Relax with a book, I expect, after I've seen the Collinses in and had something to eat. I'm starving, actually,' she added with a burst of candour. 'I haven't had anything to eat since that toast you made me this morning.'

Martin stopped outside the shower-room and turned to face her, and with a great effort of will she wrenched her eyes away and edged past towards the safety of her own room.

'So you're not going to visit your good friends in the village?' he persisted.

'No, I told you, I'm staying in,' Lorna repeated firmly, wondering why he was so curious about her movements. 'I'm quite tired, if you want to know, as well as hungry. It's been a long day, what with one thing and another,' she added perhaps more tartly than she intended.

'Quite a day,' Martin agreed pleasantly. 'So if someone were to invite you out, you'd refuse?'

'Yes—no...oh, I don't know,' Lorna said crossly. Why wouldn't he go and have his shower and leave her alone?

'Well, that's a pity,' he mused, leaning casually against the wall and eyeing her thoughtfully. 'Because I don't much care for eating alone. I do too much of it in my job, and I had hoped for some pleasant company this evening.'

Lorna frowned, puzzled. 'But Jane...?'

'Jane is busy on some new designs and, besides, it wasn't Jane who invited me to dinner last evening and opened a bottle of her father's special claret for the occasion. I had hoped to repay that hospitality, but if you'd rather stay at home with a book...?'

He shrugged and turned into the room behind him, pausing as he heard Lorna's gasp.

'You're asking *me* out to dinner?'

'That's right.'

'But I thought...' Lorna caught Martin's eye and pulled a rueful face. 'But you never said anything, not even when you asked me to book you a table—and I'd never have suggested the Galleon, not if I'd known,' she added with a pang of remorse. 'I could go and cancel it, if you like? Find somewhere cheaper.'

Martin dismissed her offer with an impatient wave of his hand. 'Of course not. As for not saying anything——' his mouth curved into a grin '—I suppose it was a bit mean, but I wanted to see what pit you'd dig for yourself this time!' He shivered suddenly and rubbed his arms. 'Goodness, I'm getting cold standing here! Go on, girl, stop havering and leave me to have my shower. I'll wait for you downstairs. Unless you'd prefer to stay in with your book?'

Lorna shook her head vigorously. 'Of course I wouldn't—and thank you very much...if you're quite sure?' There was still a small niggle of doubt that he might be teasing her.

One look at his face was enough to reassure her on that point, and she was just about to hurry off to her room when Martin called her back.

'There is one thing—call it a favour, if you like.'

'What?'

'Don't do any more thinking. No more jumping to conclusions—not of any kind. Just for this evening at least. Please?'

Lorna shot him a cheerful grin and almost danced along the corridor to her bedroom.

Her heart seemed to be playing a little game of its own, fluttering and singing inside her. Martin was taking *her* out to dinner, and after all that had happened that afternoon, and everything she'd said to him.

When was the last time she'd been taken to the Galleon? It must have been her birthday, last April, that time she'd thought Iain really was going to ask her to marry him at last. She shook her head impatiently as she caught at her thick braid to begin to unplait it. She couldn't go on waiting forever...

Still, this wasn't the moment to start thinking about that particular problem. She must get ready for her date and decide what to wear, too.

Not that there was much choice, Lorna thought ruefully as she scanned her limited wardrobe of jeans and sweaters, and mainly old ones at that. It really was time she bought something new, maybe the next time she went to Edinburgh if funds allowed. But that didn't solve the immediate problem...

All she had that seemed suitable was her kilt, a couple of cotton frocks or the dark green old faithful, the dress she'd bought for the students' reunion at St Andrews that year she'd met up with Jane again.

She'd always considered it to be a lucky dress and she knew it suited her with its full skirt and the low square-cut neck. She held it against her, noting how the colour set off her corn-coloured hair and reflected the green of her eyes, but it could hardly be called the height of sophistication.

That had never bothered her before, and she was surprised to discover that she minded so much now, but, then, it wasn't often, or ever, that she was invited out by such a sophisticated escort. That was about the last word you could apply to Iain, she thought with a private grin, and in any case he never minded nor hardly noticed what she wore.

She went into the bathroom to run her bath, swirling in a generous amount of the expensive lotion Jane had given her last Christmas and lay back soaking luxuriously in the scented water, closing her eyes tight against the sudden vision conjured up from somewhere deep in her subconscious of another naked body, male and alarmingly attractive, only just along the corridor from her.

Her toes clenched in sudden ecstasy before she forced her thoughts back to her wardrobe and found herself hankering wistfully for something really trendy to wear tonight, something that would startle Martin and show him she wasn't just a simple country girl marooned here with her ponies and her guest-house. But that was like wishing for the moon, she decided, staring morosely at her feet, for that was exactly what she was, by nature and by choice, and there was no disguising the fact.

Back in her bedroom she sat down at her dressing-table and stared unenthusiastically at her reflection in the mirror, seeing a roundish face, clear greenish eyes, slanting up at the corners... nose freckled and tiptilted, or snub if you wanted to be unkind, wide-ish mouth... It all added up to a pleasant enough, prettyish whole, Lorna thought dispassionately, a very '-ish' face altogether, in fact, and definitely no beauty.

She stretched out her arms, noting more freckles on the tanned skin, the sensible short nails on the brown fingers—fingers of an outdoor girl with no pretensions to elegance. As for her figure... Her ruthlessly self-critical gaze moved downwards. At least all her curves were reasonably well-proportioned and in all the right places. Not a lot to worry about there.

Lorna slipped the green dress over her head, relishing the almost sensuous feel of the silky material sliding over her bare skin. It was nice to have the excuse to dress up, and she gave a little twirl that swung the full skirt round her legs as she fastened the belt round her waist.

She brushed her hair till it shone, dabbed on some lipstick, then some powder in a vain attempt to disguise her freckles, and stood back to view the final effect.

Lorna frowned, tugging at the bodice which revealed rather more of her than the comfortable shirts she normally wore, reached for her bag and high-heeled sandals then, barefoot, and with her heart accelerating pleasantly, she shut her door behind her and went to find Martin.

The westering sun was slanting through the window halfway down the staircase, blinding Lorna momentarily, so that she didn't see that Martin was already standing in the hall.

Her loosened hair gleamed gold in the sunlight and the curves of her body were silhouetted against the brightness beyond the window, making Martin catch his breath as he watched her descent, the unmistakable physical response that surged through him taking him by surprise.

Instinctively he moved forward out of the shadows.

'Martin! I haven't kept you waiting, have I?' Lorna glanced at her watch as she came down the last few steps. 'It's not time to leave yet, is it?'

Her cheeks flushed as she registered the look of undisguised admiration in the bright blue eyes, and she saw that he, too, had changed for the occasion. He was wearing a soft black leather jacket that seemed by the very suppleness of the skin to emphasise the hardness of the broad shoulders beneath—shoulders she had seen naked only a short time before, she remembered with a little *frisson* of excitement.

Her pulse quickened as he drew nearer and reached out to lift her hand to his lips, holding her eyes with his.

'You look very different,' he commented with audible approval in his deep voice.

'It's not surprising.' Lorna managed a rather shaky laugh. 'I feel different too—especially my legs which live almost permanently in jeans. They feel as if they've been let out of prison.'

Martin's gaze travelled slowly down the length of her body to the limbs in question, resting briefly in passing on the gentle swell revealed by the low neckline of her dress and making Lorna acutely conscious of the racing heartbeats she was convinced were only too visible.

'I'm glad you've—er—released them, temporarily at least, from their confinement,' Martin murmured with a twitch of his lips. 'But are your feet joining them in their bid for freedom?'

Lorna giggled and waved the sandals. 'No, I do have shoes. I'm not sure whether bare feet would be quite the thing for an evening out, and I'll put them on when the taxi arrives, although . . .'

She frowned and bit her lip, weighing up Martin's likely reaction to the idea which had just occurred to her.

'Although what?'

'Although,' Lorna said slowly, 'it does seem rather an unnecessary luxury to have a taxi to take us to Tobermory and collect us when I could perfectly well drive us. Should I see whether I could cancel it? Unless you have a particular aversion to Land Rovers?' she added, glaring at him defiantly in anticipation of a repeat of his sarcastic remarks on the subject of her vehicle.

But Martin did not rise to the bait.

'Wouldn't you prefer to go by taxi?' he enquired mildly. 'Wouldn't it make a change for you? Of course if I had my own car...' He shrugged.

'We'd be freer if I drove, though, and we wouldn't have to hurry back if you wanted to look round Tobermory after we'd had dinner. Let me see, anyway—of course, it might be too late. Duncan may have already left...

'That's settled, then,' Lorna told Martin, putting down the phone a moment or two later. 'And you won't mind taking the risk of travelling with me—you're not afraid I might not be able to control my Land Rover, are you?' She stared up at him, all wide-eyed innocence, accentuating her Scottish accent. 'It's a very unwieldy vehicle for a mere girl to handle, and the roads are awful narrow.'

Martin drew in his breath sharply, and for an instant Lorna remembered that glimpse she'd had of his temper. Had she gone too far? The opportunity to get her own back had been too good to resist.

'I see I'm not going to be forgiven easily for that remark,' Martin countered drily, 'and if I were of a more suspicious nature, I might even think you wanted to cancel the taxi to prove a point—but,' he added in a lower voice as he closed the gap between them, 'being of a suspicious nature yourself you'd never believe me if I told you I regret my car being out of action simply because I'd prefer to chauffeur you myself. And not for any chauvinistic reasons, either, but that dress isn't meant——'

The end of his sentence was abruptly curtailed by a ring at the front door and Lorna didn't know whether to be glad or sorry she would never hear his description of her dress although she thought—hoped, even—she could guess the drift of what he had been about to say.

She opened the door, aware that she hardly presented a picture of a typical landlady, and smiled cheerfully at the middle-aged couple on her doorstep.

'Miss Morrison?' the woman began uncertainly. 'We rang earlier, but maybe we got the wrong...?'

'Mr and Mrs Collins? Please, do come in. I was expecting you, and your room is all ready.'

Two pairs of eyes tried not to look too disconcerted at her glamorous appearance, and Lorna went on quickly with a reassuring grin. 'I don't usually dress like this, but I'm being taken out to dinner this evening.'

'That's nice,' Mrs Collins returned, 'and you look very——'

'Fetching,' her husband put in, 'if you don't mind my saying so.'

'Very fetching,' Martin murmured under his breath as Lorna passed him, making her heart lift on a bubble of air.

She showed the Collinses to their room but they followed her downstairs almost immediately.

'We'll unpack later,' Mrs Collins explained. 'It's such a lovely evening we want to make the most of our time here and do some exploring before the sun goes down.'

'Come back any time,' Lorna said, giving them a front-door key. 'And if I'm not back, just make yourselves at home—oh, and the kitchen's through there if you want to make a hot drink.'

* * *

'Perhaps we could do some exploring too?' Martin suggested as he climbed into the Land Rover beside Lorna not long afterwards. 'Now you know I'm not here for any nefarious purpose you might be willing to show me round a bit—unless you still want to keep your island to yourself,' he added lightly, 'and not want to share its charms with anyone, even me.'

Lorna shot him a wary glance, but he seemed perfectly serious as he settled into his seat and did up the safety-belt. She switched on the engine and drove slowly out of the stable-yard and down the track leading to the road.

'Of course I don't, nor do any of us. We like sharing it with anybody so long as they appreciate it. It's only... Well, I won't go into all that again. You know my feelings on the subject.' She grinned wryly at him. 'Only too well, I imagine.'

She waved one hand expansively at the rolling moorland ahead of them. 'Just look at that view,' she ordered him. 'Isn't it beautiful, and can you blame me for wanting to keep it unspoilt?'

A stream, glinting gold in the mellow light, meandered through the little glen, from which her house got its name, bordered by birches and rowan trees whose berries glowed scarlet in the sun, and Lorna knew that if she turned the engine off there would be no man-made sound to disturb the tranquillity.

Martin followed her gaze and nodded. 'No,' he said slowly, 'I can't, but life does go on, you know. Things change. This landscape, for instance; it wasn't always as empty as this, was it? Before the Clearances it would have been full of crofters and their animals.'

'You know about all that?'

'That book of yours I'm reading describes it in graphic detail—how the Highlanders were evicted from their homes and land to make way for sheep.'

'And what's happening to the sheep now? And the people?' Lorna's hands clenched fiercely on the steering-wheel and her eyes flashed emerald sparks of anger as she answered herself. 'The original crofters emigrated to Canada and Australia, and now their descendants are being pushed aside again. You only have to look at those furrows on the hillside. It's forests now, not sheep.'

She turned to Martin and was brought up sharp by his quizzical expression. 'Oh, dear, was I going on again?'

He nodded with a grin. 'Just a bit. I do understand how you feel, you know. You've made it pretty plain.'

There was a short pause, then Lorna heard a heavy sigh. 'I was looking forward to a pleasant drive and a good meal with amusing and light-hearted conversation, strictly uncontroversial—though if you did want an argument I could point out the illogicality of some of your reasoning. That development you're so worried about—that would help keep people here, wouldn't it?'

'Don't let's start on that again,' Lorna said hastily, 'or we might both regret it.' She pulled a face at him. 'It was you who asked me to keep off my hobby-horse, if you recall, so it's not fair to goad it at the same time.'

Martin touched her knee lightly. 'Poor Lorna. It's going to be a very frustrating evening for you. Whatever will we find to talk about?' His voice dropped as he went on, 'I know what I'd like to talk about—I want to find out more about a certain energetic and rather unusual landlady.'

Lorna kept her eyes firmly on the road ahead, feeling his hand increase its pressure before he removed it from her knee. 'I thought you wanted me to tell you about the island,' she returned as steadily as she could. 'Look—that's one of my favourite places, that loch over there.'

She slowed down to point it out. 'There's a lovely walk all round it, and you can get down to the shore through a gully at the end. I could show you one day, if you like?'

She glanced across at Martin, expecting to find him gazing out of the window in the direction in which she was pointing, but instead found his eyes fixed firmly on her own face.

'You're supposed to be looking at the countryside,' she scolded him, trying to retain her composure under his unwavering scrutiny, 'and taking in the local attractions.'

'Oh, I am,' he said softly, leaning back in his seat with every sign of enjoyment. 'I really am, believe me.'

Lorna began to feel strangely light-headed but put it down to the fact that she had scarcely eaten all day. Even so, it didn't take a genius to know what lay behind Martin's banter, and the knowledge that he was finding her attractive brought an added sparkle to her eyes and a new zest to her conversation as she persevered with her PR job on the delights of the island and its main town which they were just approaching.

'Tobermory.' At last she seemed to have caught his attention. 'Isn't that where a Spanish ship sank after the Armada? Full of undiscovered treasure, isn't it?'

'So the rumour goes,' Lorna nodded, 'and it sounds all nice and romantic, doesn't it? But actually it's not a very pretty story at all. I'll tell you about it some time, but it'd be a pity to spoil a beautiful evening with tales of darkest treachery and double-dealing.'

They rounded a corner and Lorna slackened speed as they drove along a narrow road which widened out as it came into the little port.

'Here it is—look.'

Lorna parked by the quay heaped with fishing-nets and lobster-pots and watched Martin stare round at the tranquil scene before him and shake his head in disbelief.

'For such a small and peaceful-looking island it does seem extraordinarily subject to turmoil and violence of one sort and another,' he commented. 'Passions clearly run very high hereabouts.' He caught Lorna's eye and she grinned.

'Ah, well, we Celts are an ancient and passionate race,' she told him, bending down to remove her driving shoes and glancing sideways up at him.

Martin raised one eyebrow. 'So I've noticed,' he remarked drily. 'And just to put the record straight, I also lay claim to Celtic blood and can be as passionate as the next man—or woman—when I'm roused.'

There was a short, pregnant pause and Lorna kept her head studiously turned away as her fingers struggled with the buckles of her sandals. Was his remark a warning—or a promise? His tone gave nothing away, but this certainly wasn't the moment to put it to the test.

She slid out of the Land Rover and began to lead the way along what in a larger resort would be called the promenade.

There weren't many people about, mainly holidaymakers in their casual gear, and Lorna suddenly felt rather conspicuous tripping along on her high-heels and in decidedly uncasual clothes, accompanied by her tall, elegant escort.

She flicked a surreptitious glance sideways and felt her heart bang uncomfortably against her ribs. Martin's dark hair just brushed the collar of his soft leather jacket and her hand clenched as she fought off a sudden insane urge to reach up and caress those small, tantalising curls lying against his neck, to touch the smoothness of his cheek now in profile as he walked beside her.

She felt as though she were walking on air, and for one disloyal moment she found herself comparing Martin's dark good looks with Iain's homely features, too familiar to cause this leaping pulse or the elated anticipation that lightened her step.

Horrified, she wrenched her thoughts, and her eyes, away from the danger zone. What was she thinking of? There was no comparison between the two men, none at all.

She hurried on, pulled back to earth—literally—by Martin's hand grasping her elbow. Startled, she swung round to meet his amused expression.

'This is the restaurant, I take it? I can't see any other called the Galleon.'

Lorna nodded. 'Yes, sorry! I was miles away.'

'Come on, then, let's go and eat.' Martin's fingers tightened, sending a delightful tremor running through her body, and then, keeping her arm firmly locked in his possessive grip, he turned and ushered her through the door.

CHAPTER FIVE

LORNA couldn't help darting an anxious look round as they were shown to their table. Supposing someone who knew her and Iain saw her with Martin?

Not that there was anything to feel guilty about, dining here with another man—and he was only a casual acquaintance, after all. Even so, she couldn't help worrying just a little that if Iain was to find out . . .

'Something wrong?'

Lorna refocused her eyes on Martin's face with an apologetic smile.

'Sorry—no, of course not. Everything's fine, really fine,' she added emphatically as she reassured herself that there was nobody in the restaurant she knew even slightly. Even Tony, the proprietor, must be having a night off.

She sat back in her chair with a contented sigh, knowing she could relax, now that even that little cloud had lifted, and perused the menu wondering what to choose from the selection of delicious-sounding dishes.

'I'm not sure this isn't the best part of eating out,' she confided. 'I think the anticipation's more enjoyable than the food itself.'

Martin laughed. 'You're a very rewarding person to take out,' he told her, 'and for the life of me I can't understand why every man on the island isn't queueing up to do just that. Or maybe they are, and they're hiding away somewhere waiting their turn.'

'That's right,' Lorna said airily. 'I come here every week, actually. It almost gets boring.'

While the waiter was taking their order she sat back and watched Martin, thinking how utterly self-assured he was, and once again she had to shake her head to rid it of that intrusive image of Iain that would insist on slipping into her thoughts, calling up an unbidden comparison of his gentle, rather diffident manner with Martin's far more commanding presence.

This time, though, Martin seemed not to have noticed her lapse of concentration as he discussed the choice of wine with their waiter.

'I've chosen a Chablis,' he told her. 'I hope you'll like it. I thought it would go well with the seafood we've ordered.'

Seafood was the Galleon's speciality, and they had both opted for Scotch salmon *en croute* in a delicate herb sauce with new potatoes and a selection of fresh vegetables.

'Lovely.' She smiled happily and leant back, her eyes sparkling across the table at her host. 'I can't wait. I really am starving, and the wine will probably go straight to my head. Maybe we should have had that taxi after all.'

Martin smiled. 'It's very light, not at all like that splendid claret we had last night.' He hesitated as his face grew grave. 'Your father?' he asked tentatively. 'Is he...?'

He let the words trail away into a questioning silence and Lorna nodded, reaching for a roll which she crumbled between her fingers.

'He died when I'd just started at college. That must be about, oh, six or seven years ago now, I suppose. He was in the merchant navy and caught some virus out East, and he died before they could get him home.'

'I'm sorry,' Martin said quietly. 'I shouldn't have asked. It's none of my business.'

'It doesn't matter. We've got over it now.' Lorna smiled gently. 'It's quite nice to talk about him, actually. He was a very special man, and I'm only sad I saw so little of him. He was away such a lot, though when he did come home it was like one long party.' Her eyes shone reminiscently. 'He was so *alive* and so interested in everything.'

'Including wine,' Martin observed, pouring her a glass from the bottle which had just arrived at their table.

'Including wine.' Lorna took a sip and nodded appreciatively. 'This is delicious—thanks.'

Their starters came then and the mood changed as they both tucked in with relish, Lorna to an avocado mousse and Martin to an exotic-looking seafood cocktail.

'Isn't this lovely?' Lorna sighed contentedly after a while. 'I get so fed up with making meals just for myself and it's a great temptation not to bother when I get in hot and tired after a long ride.'

'What makes you do it?' Martin asked curiously. 'It's been intriguing me ever since I arrived at Glenmore.' He finished the last of his sauce and pushed the dish away to rest his elbows on the table. 'What made you choose such a hard and probably not all that profitable life when so many other careers would be open to you, especially with a degree?'

Lorna's chin lifted stubbornly. 'You sound just like my mother. Her arthritis forced her to leave and go and live in Edinburgh, and she's always trying to persuade me to go and join her and get what she calls a "proper" job.'

She finished her mousse and sat back to meet Martin's interested gaze. 'It's quite simple,' she went on. 'I love Glenmore more than anything in the world, and I just couldn't imagine living—or working—anywhere else. It's been in our family for generations and if I didn't look after it, there's no one else. I've got no brothers or sisters, you see.'

'You could let it,' Martin suggested reasonably.

'And worry all the time that it wasn't being properly looked after? No, thanks,' Lorna replied fiercely.

Martin grinned. 'You talk about your home almost as though it were a person.'

Lorna's eyes wandered thoughtfully through the window to the yachts floating in the harbour. 'Maybe I do,' she said slowly. 'Rather like the way some people feel about ships.'

'And how do you see the future?' Martin persisted, moving slightly to let the waiter take the plates but never shifting his eyes from her face. 'Are you planning to stay here for the rest of your life, taking in guests and running your pony-trekking business? What happens if you want to get married? Your husband might have something to say about that.'

Lorna shrugged and spread her hands. 'I hope any man who really loved me wouldn't expect me to make that sort of choice.'

Her face set into a mulish expression and Martin let the matter drop, and for a while they talked of other, less personal matters as they had the evening before.

'That was delicious.' Lorna heaved a sigh of utter contentment as she regretfully came to the final mouthful of her salmon. 'I think it was an even better meal than the last time I came here.'

'And when was that? Recently?'

Lorna shook her head and pushed her hair back impatiently over her shoulders. 'Last April, on my birthday.'

'You didn't come alone, I assume?' Martin raised one eyebrow and made as though to pour the last of the wine into her glass, but Lorna covered it quickly with her hand.

'Not for me, thanks. I don't want to be arrested on the way home, and to lose my licence would be about the worst thing that could happen to me.'

Martin emptied the bottle into his own glass. 'You haven't answered my question,' he reminded her.

'No, I didn't come alone,' Lorna answered evenly. 'A friend brought me.'

'A "good" friend?'

Lorna stared steadily at him across the table, wide-eyed and solemn. 'A very good and old friend, by way of being a birthday present.'

She saw a gleam flicker in the sea-blue gaze holding her own and decided the time had come to do some probing of her own.

'And you, Mr Ritchie,' she retaliated with a bright smile, 'tell me about yourself. I think you've discovered quite enough about me, but all I know about you is that you're a director of a tour company based in Glasgow. Do you live there too? Is that where you come from originally?'

'Yes and no. Yes, I live there now, but my roots are in Northumberland, near Alnwick.' It was his turn to gaze out of the window. 'It's beautiful there, not unlike your island, though wilder.'

'And do you have family there, still?'

'My parents and my sister. She's married to a farmer, and I go back there whenever I can, though these days that's not very often.' He grinned suddenly. 'Even Sassenach tour directors can lay claim to sentimental feelings about their particular piece of land, you see. Now, what about some desert, and coffee?'

Lorna eyed the sweet-trolley longingly. 'I shouldn't, I suppose, but it all looks too good to resist, doesn't it?'

'Definitely,' Martin returned firmly, 'and from where I'm sitting I can't see any reason why you should feel you have to resist anything!'

His eyes lingered admiringly on her trim figure, causing another blush to colour her cheeks. Lorna put her hand to her face.

'And you don't need to worry about that, either,' Martin continued softly. 'It does wonders for your complexion!'

Thankfully for her composure, the waiter appeared just then, but, while Martin was talking to him, Lorna found herself wondering, with a little spurt of apprehension, just how the evening might end.

Would Martin kiss her, and did she want him to? And if he did kiss her, would it just be a goodnight peck on the cheek, or something more?

Instinctively her eyes strayed to Martin's mouth, firm and decisive, noticing for the first time the sensually inviting curve to his lower lip, and deep down, however she tried to disguise or suppress it, Lorna knew the response was there within her, waiting... hoping, even...

Perhaps it was a good thing she would be in the driving-seat on the way home—literally—just in case.

'I did enjoy that,' she said with a regretful backward glance as they left the restaurant a little later. 'Thank you so much. It's been a lovely evening.'

They crossed the road and Lorna stopped to lean on the railings overlooking the harbour and gazed idly at the lights reflected in the gently moving water.

It was high tide and little waves splashed against the stone wall beneath them, and it was dark enough now for a few stars to have appeared in the translucent sky.

You couldn't have wished for a more romantic scene, Lorna thought dreamily. Even the soft music was there, wafting across faintly from one of the big yachts anchored further out. All that was missing was the tall dark hero murmuring sweet nothings into her ear, his strong arm stealing round her waist...

She glanced round with a smile, expecting to find Martin just behind her, but he wasn't even looking at her. In fact, he seemed totally impervious to the enchantments of the view and was standing a little way off with his back to the sea as he stared thoughtfully round at his surroundings.

'It's quite an attractive place, isn't it?' he remarked, sounding quite surprised. 'Is there anything else to see, apart from this?'

He made a sweeping gesture with his arm, as though to embrace the line of buildings fronting the little port, before thrusting his hands back into his pockets. 'I was wondering whether my clients would like to come here. What are the hotels like? Is there anywhere in the luxury class where they could stay?'

His eyes came to rest queryingly on Lorna's face and she bridled at once. 'There are several hotels, but I really couldn't say whether they'd come up to your clients' demanding expectations. They are obviously very particular people.'

She couldn't help her tone being coloured by her disappointment at the way the evening seemed to be ending, and saw Martin's eyebrows rise at the sharpness of her tone.

Just then a breeze ruffled the surface of the water, fragmenting the reflected lights and brushing her bare arms so that she gave an involuntary shiver.

Martin took a step towards her. 'You're cold,' he observed. 'Come on, I mustn't keep you out here chatting. Let's go back. I can always come and have a scout round on my own once I get the Merc back.'

They walked along in silence, a few feet apart, and climbed back into the Land Rover with barely a word between them.

Even when their hands touched as they reached down to do up their safety-belts, Martin gave no sign that he had even noticed the brief physical contact.

It was as if the almost flirtatious light-heartedness of the earlier part of the evening had never been, and Lorna's heart felt like lead.

'Thank you again for this evening,' she said as brightly as she could. 'I'm sure I've eaten far too much, but I really enjoyed myself.'

'I enjoyed myself, too,' Martin replied, his even tone giving nothing away. 'And I'm glad I was able to repay your hospitality.'

'My efforts were hardly in the same league,' Lorna returned with a light laugh, thinking they both might have been composing thank-you notes. 'But I did appreciate it.'

She turned on the engine and set off along the street to make the return journey to Glenmore, wondering dismally whatever she could have said to cause this apparent coolness that had sprung up between them.

Or was she just imagining it? After all, there was no reason at all why Martin should want to kiss her, especially after the way she'd spoken to him only that afternoon. They were scarcely more than strangers to one another, and she mustn't let a few appreciative glances go to her head. He'd be off in a day or two, back to Glasgow and...

Of course! How could she have been so blind?

The Land Rover swerved violently, threatening to leave the road, as the realisation of the truth stabbed home.

Martin was married, or engaged! Or at the very least there'd be a girlfriend waiting for him, an attractive and successful man as he was, already, she guessed, in his early thirties.

What a mercy she hadn't thrown herself at him and made a complete fool of herself.

'Lorna?'

'Martin...'

Simultaneously their voices broke the silence and Lorna felt Martin's eyes on her as she steadied the Land Rover.

'Are you OK?' he asked, sounding concerned.

Lorna nodded and shook back her hair. 'Sorry about that. I...I thought I saw something back there...a rabbit, probably. I swerved to avoid it,' she ended lamely.

'I see. Your eyes are sharper than mine,' Martin observed drily. 'I can't say I noticed anything. Still, no damage done.'

'No.'

Another silence fell between them, then Martin spoke again. 'Shall we stop for a moment? There's something I ought to tell you.'

Lorna's heart plummeted. This was it. What else could be so important that he needed her to stop to tell her?

Biting her lip, she drove on a short way, then pulled the big vehicle over on to the grass verge overlooking the small loch she'd pointed out to Martin earlier. She turned the engine off and sat quite still, keeping her eyes fixed straight ahead and noticing, as though for the first time, the steep hill on the far side of the water, dense black against the night sky, its exactly mirrored reflection only disturbed by the silver circles of a rising fish.

'So what's worrying you?' Martin asked quietly. 'You've hardly spoken since we left the restaurant.'

Lorna bent her head, her thick hair curtaining her face from his questioning eyes. 'I'm not worried. I just had something on my mind. Nothing important—honestly.'

'Important enough to stop you talking—just when we'd been enjoying each other's company and getting to know one another. At least I thought so. Did I say something to upset you?'

'No, no. Nothing like that.' Lorna shook her head vehemently.

'You're not worrying about the development rumour again? Or harbouring more suspicions about me?'

Lorna managed a laugh. 'No, not that either. Please, don't bother about it. It's nothing.'

'Mmm.' Martin didn't sound in the least convinced, but how could she tell him what was really on her mind? Or ask him straight out whether he was married or not? It shouldn't be any concern of hers, anyway, as she kept trying to convince herself.

Then she gasped as Martin leant across and moved aside the heavy locks of hair with warm, strong fingers that brushed across her cheek.

'That's better,' he murmured. 'I can just see you now.'

She felt her body sway towards him, almost against her will, as his lips came lightly down on hers before he drew back again to search her face in the darkness for her response.

Whatever it was he saw in her shining eyes seemed to satisfy him, for he took her chin again in firm, hard fingers which allowed no escape, running his thumb softly over her mouth as though preparing it for the demands of his own.

Her pulse began to race in uneven beats as slowly and surely his lips took possession of hers in a long, lingering kiss that made her body tremble in the strong arms that held her.

At last he let her go, but not for long.

'This isn't the ideal place for dalliance,' he murmured with a chuckle into her hair as he reached down to unfasten their safety-belts. He slipped one arm behind her then to draw her closer. 'But I'm not complaining,' he added quickly, 'just in case you think I'm about to cast aspersions on your precious Land Rover.'

'I didn't buy it with dalliance in mind,' Lorna managed to say before his mouth covered hers again, sensuously warm as it moved to travel over her face, her throat...her neck... while his hand roved down over her body till at last it came to rest on the curves of her breast.

Lorna felt his finger begin to stroke the bare skin swelling above the deep neckline of her dress and hardly dared moved for the ecstasy that swept over her, making her respond to his caresses with an urgency that took her by surprise as she pressed against the taut muscles of his chest.

How long she sat in the darkness rapturously locked in Martin's embrace she couldn't have said—a minute, an hour... Time ceased to have any meaning. Now was all that mattered.

She let out the softest of sighs as she reached up shyly to touch the smooth, firm skin of Martin's cheek, moving her hand round to where the thick hair curled into his neck, remembering how she'd wanted to do that earlier.

She heard a low laugh as Martin reached for her hand and brought it back to his lips, kissing each finger in turn.

'You never said what it was you wanted me to stop for,' Lorna reminded him in a muffled voice. It wasn't easy to speak clearly with your face pressed against a man's chest. 'You said you wanted to tell me something.'

'I did, didn't I?' Amusement danced in the deep voice somewhere above her head. 'I'm not sure I can remember exactly,' he teased. 'Somehow I seem to have got sidetracked, but I think it was something to do with telling you I wanted to kiss you. I've been wanting to all evening, but I was waiting for somewhere a bit more private than the main street outside the restaurant where everyone could see us.'

His arm tightened round her. 'Not that there's anything to be ashamed of in a man giving a girl a goodnight kiss, but it is your home town, and I didn't know how many curious eyes and wagging tongues there might be hidden behind all those curtains.'

'Oh, Martin.' Lorna began to feel absurdly happy and rather foolish, too. 'So it wasn't because...'

'Because what?'

'Because you're married—or something?' she blurted out, grateful that the darkness hid her blushing cheeks.

'Not even "or something",' Martin assured her gravely. 'A rolling stone and fancy free, that's me. A girl in every island, but definitely no wife.'

Lorna giggled. 'That must keep you busy.'

'Oh, it does, very,' came the grave reply, followed by a stifled groan. 'But I don't have to keep many of my assignations in a Land Rover, Miss Morrison.' Martin tried to stretch out his legs and disentangled his arm reluctantly from behind her shoulders. 'I'm sorry, and I know it's the height of ungallantry, as well as being extremely unromantic, but I think I'll have to get out for a minute. I'm getting cramp!'

He uncoiled his long limbs and slipped out into the darkness, leaving Lorna to watch his tall, shadowy figure in an agony of indecision.

Should she get out too and go and join him on the pretext of needing to ease her own stiffening joints—which wouldn't be true—or would he see through that lame excuse to the real reason behind her action? That what she was really doing was giving him the chance to take her in his arms again out there in the night, free from the restricting confines of the Land Rover?

The whole of her body began to ache for his embrace and she felt her heart begin to thud painfully against her ribs as she wrapped her arms round herself as though to calm it down, only to sense it leap again as she watched Martin come slowly round to open her door and hold out his hand to her in a wordless invitation.

Strong arms encircled her waist, supported her, then drew her close.

'That's better,' he whispered into her hair. 'As I said, Land Rovers may have their good points, but their design leaves a lot to be desired in one respect. It's funny, but my cramp seems to have disappeared altogether!'

Lorna felt a blissful shudder run through her as Martin's hands roamed hungrily over her body, lingering on every curve with urgently sensuous caresses, and she reached up to wind her arms round his neck, offering her face for the kiss which came swiftly down on to her lips, almost crushing the breath from her.

Her stomach ached with a tortured yearning as she responded willingly to the movements of his hands and she seemed to have lost all power to resist, even had she wanted to.

'Oh, Lorna, you're beautiful!'

Martin's voice sounded strangely husky and Lorna clung tightly to him, pressing her cheek to his pounding heart.

His arms tightened almost convulsively round her then suddenly their hold slackened and he stepped back a pace, holding her a little away from him as he looked tenderly down into her face.

'I think we'd better go back,' he said, not quite steadily, 'or I won't be answerable for my actions, and I'm not sure this is quite the place for...'

He left the words unsaid and touched her hair, twining his fingers through the thick tresses till they came to rest on the slender stem of her neck. Then he bent to crush her mouth with his for one final kiss—warm, passionate and urgent with desire.

Lorna heard a sort of moan escape her as she melted against him and she knew there would be no holding back if he should demand more of her, but, even as the thought raced through her mind, he drew back and placed one hand on her waist to guide her gently back towards the waiting vehicle.

She stopped and looked up at him. 'Martin, could you drive us home?' she asked, not quite steadily. 'I feel a bit drunk, and I don't think it's the wine. I'm not sure I'd be safe, just at the moment, after...'

Lorna waved her hand weakly, incapable of describing the dizzying effect of the past moments, and Martin caught it to lead her round to the passenger side where he helped her up into her seat.

'No trouble, Cinderella,' he smiled. 'Actually, it's quite a relief to know you're willing to let someone else take charge just once in a while. Even superwomen have to hand over the reins sometimes.'

Lorna was too bemused and too happy even to think up a suitable retort, and leant her head back, thinking how comforting it was to be taken care of just occasionally.

She must have dozed off for it was with quite a start that she came to a little later and realised that they had come to a halt in her own stable-yard.

'This is where you usually park, isn't it?' Martin asked as he waited for her to struggle upright.

'This is fine—thanks. And thanks again for a lovely evening,' she added shyly, seeing Martin's face more clearly now in the light from the kitchen window. 'But there's something...' The words drifted to an uncertain halt as she met Martin's quizzical smile.

'What's bothering you now?' he asked indulgently.

'It's just that after all I said to you this afternoon in the shop——' she waved her hand towards it '—I can't imagine why you wanted to take me out, and spend the evening with me. Most people would have left on the spot and not treated me to dinner and...and everything...'

'Ah, but I'm not most people, am I? And you're not like any girl I've ever met, either. I couldn't leave the island without trying to get to know you better.'

Their eyes met and held, then he leant across to kiss her softly, just once, before getting out and coming round to open her door.

'I think your other guests are already back,' he said, nodding towards another car parked in the far corner, and his hand tightened round hers as they stood together in the deep shadow cast by the wall of the house.

A small sigh escaped Lorna's parted lips raised for his goodnight kiss—a sigh of regret mingled with a tinge of relief. Her emotions were in such turmoil she knew she dared not trust herself to make the right response to any further demands Martin might make on her. She needed time and space to come to terms with everything that had happened to her since they had left Glenmore earlier that evening, and the Collinses' presence in the house would guarantee just that.

She led the way into the kitchen and pulled the back door to sharply, saying in a loud and, she hoped, normal voice for the benefit of anyone within earshot, 'So if there's nothing more you need, Martin, I'll say good-night to Mr and Mrs Collins, then I'll be away to my bed.'

She grinned mischievously up at him as his eyes glinted dangerously.

'There may be nothing I need, Miss Morrison, but wanting is a different matter.'

He made as if to pull her into his arms again, but Lorna managed to slip past him and out of the door leading to the hall.

There was no one about, but she could hear Mr and Mrs Collins talking and moving about upstairs, so she turned off the lights and began to climb the staircase, pausing halfway up to look down into Martin's up-turned face.

'I'll say goodnight, then,' she said softly, 'and thanks again for a most enjoyable evening. I hope you sleep well.'

Then, without waiting for his reply, she turned and ran quickly up to her own room and shut the door firmly behind her.

CHAPTER SIX

CONTRARY to all her expectations, Lorna fell asleep at once and only awoke with a start when the alarm jangled in her ear at six-thirty the following morning.

For a while she lay in a kind of blissful trance between sleep and full wakefulness, dimly aware that something out of the ordinary had happened recently, but not quite able to recollect what it was.

Then she remembered. Martin. With a smile she turned on to her back, her fingers straying to her mouth as though she might still be able to feel the lingering imprint of his lips.

Something deep within her stirred at the memory of being held in his arms and she lay quite still, afraid that the slightest movement might obliterate the delicious sensation for ever. Then she remembered something else, too. Today might be Martin's last day here at Glenmore. If Archie had got the part for the Mercedes he'd be off and away today or tomorrow, leaving her with only the evening's memories and an empty room to tidy and prepare for another guest.

She knew she must be sensible, and not get carried away by what had, after all, been nothing but a brief romantic interlude between two people who hardly knew one another. What was it he'd said? 'A girl on every island'? Lorna sighed. Even if it had only been said as a joke, Martin might well have intended her to take it as a gentle warning that he wasn't the sort of man who wanted ties or any permanent relationships—a real rolling stone.

In any case, what was she thinking of? It was she who had a permanent relationship, with Iain. Martin could mean nothing to her, not in that way. Iain... Lorna conjured up his kind, comfortable features, but, as she curled up under the duvet and wrapped her arms tightly round her body, she realised with a jolt that Iain's kisses had never set her on fire as Martin's had done, nor had his gentle embrace ever aroused such sensations in her body, which even now tensed deliciously at the memory of Martin's caresses.

It was like being given a taste of champagne after a lifetime's diet of bread and water, she thought extravagantly. You knew you couldn't have more than a glassful, but that made it all the more desirable when the bottle was about to be removed for ever.

She was almost relieved that Martin came down for breakfast at the same time as Mr and Mrs Collins, so that she was able to address him in the same businesslike, friendly manner with which she treated all her guests, giving herself time to suppress the agitation his appearance had re-awoken in her heart.

In fact, she went so far as to avoid his direct gaze altogether, dropping her eyes as she served his breakfast and making her escape as soon as she could to relieve her pent-up emotions in an orgy of housework.

She was cleaning the lounge when Martin put his head round the door a little later. His voice, loud above the vacuum cleaner, made her jump and she swung round with a startled grin.

'I'm off to see Archie,' he told her, then, as she switched the machine off, he edged further into the room to take up his favourite position, leaning against the wall with his hands thrust deep in his pockets. 'I want to find out the state of play down there.'

'You could ring,' Lorna pointed out. 'Save yourself a long walk.'

Martin smiled, making Lorna's heart play disturbing tricks which she did her best to ignore.

'Only yesterday you were trying to persuade me to have just that,' he reminded her. 'Today that's exactly what I do feel like, though it would be even better if you were to come with me. It's a lovely day,' he added temptingly.

'I know.' Lorna rubbed vaguely at a spot on the table nearby and pulled a face. 'I'd love to——' more than anything, she added silently '—but there's so much to do here, as well as a ride to get ready for this afternoon. I'd better not.'

Martin's eyes softened. 'That's a shame, but don't work too hard, will you? All work and no play, you know... It's not good for you. Oh, that reminds me...'

He straightened up swiftly and with a couple of long strides covered the distance between them, reaching out to pull her close and press his lips to hers in a brief, warm kiss. Then, almost as quickly, he turned, grinning over his shoulder at her expression of wide-eyed bewilderment.

'See you later,' he said cheerfully. *'Ciao!'*

'Ciao,' Lorna echoed weakly, but he'd already gone, and seconds later she heard the sound of the front door being pulled to... then silence.

Absently her hand touched her mouth as she stood for a moment, motionless, before catching sight of her pink-cheeked reflection in the mirror over the mantelpiece.

'Come on, girl,' she murmured to it rather shamefacedly. 'Keep your mind on the job and for goodness' sake stop behaving like a lovesick schoolgirl! You're a businesswoman, remember, with work to do.'

Determinedly she buckled to once more, but it all took longer than she had anticipated and, even after she'd finished the housework, there was still a lot to do outside—the ponies to bring in and their tack to check, and she should sweep the yard, too. There wouldn't be time when Fiona came to help her saddle up.

An hour later, Lorna collapsed on to a stool in the corner of the tack-room, leaning her forehead against the broom handle in a sudden wave of weariness.

'Don't work too hard,' Martin had told her. Chance would be a fine thing! Did he imagine Glenmore ran itself? No doubt he had armies of secretaries and assistants at his beck and call. He could eat out whenever he felt like it, and send his washing to a laundry—luxuries beyond her own imaginings.

Glenmore, on the other hand . . . its very existence and her own livelihood were entirely dependent on her own efforts, and hers alone. How could he be expected to understand? Fiona's meagre wages were all she could afford. Any more help was quite out of the question.

Lorna leant back against the stone wall behind her and closed her eyes. If working all the hours God sent were the price of keeping Glenmore going, then so be it.

'So this is where you've been hiding. I've been looking everywhere for you.'

Lorna's drooping lids flew open and she shaded her eyes with her hand to stare up at the figure silhouetted against the light.

'Oh, Martin! You gave me quite a fright. I never heard you coming.'

She began to struggle to her feet, and Martin quickly came across, holding out his hand to pull her up.

'You didn't see me because you were asleep,' he remarked sternly, slipping his hand under her elbow. 'I know, because I watched you for quite a few minutes before I was mean enough to wake you up. And why, may I ask, were you asleep in the middle of a beautiful, sunny day? Because you're tired, Lorna Morrison. You work too hard.'

Lorna tried to pull her arm away but felt Martin's fingers close more tightly round it.

'It could be,' she replied pertly, 'that *if* I dropped off for a second—and I'm not admitting that I did—it might be because I was kept up late last night.'

'It could be,' Martin agreed mildly, 'but it wasn't. We weren't late, not by anyone's standards. It was barely ten o'clock when we got in. So that excuse won't wash.'

Lorna managed to wriggle free at last and put the broom back in the corner, brushing her dusty hands against her jeans before pushing back a stray tendril that had escaped from her plait.

'If I want to sit down for a minute, I don't need an excuse,' she said, with a toss of her head. 'And if I work hard, that's up to me, though it's kind of you to be so concerned for my well-being.'

She glanced meaningfully at her watch. Just time to tidy up and grab a snack before Fiona came, she calculated as she started off in the direction of the house.

'How did you get on?' she asked Martin over her shoulder. 'Any news of the car?'

'You were right about your friend Archie,' Martin admitted, catching up with her. 'He really does seem to know what he's doing. He's got the part, and says the car should be ready tomorrow morning. So this is my last day here.'

'I see.'

Lorna's heart dropped. It was what she'd been expecting, but hearing him say it, and so matter-of-factly, brought home to her just what his departure would mean. She stared bleakly at the view across the moors, unaware of the slight lift of the dark eyebrows on the face studying her own, the small smile curving his mouth.

'Oh, well,' she said colourlessly. 'I expect you'll be glad to be able to get back to your own work. It must have been very frustrating for you being held up for so long.'

'Very,' Martin agreed lightly. 'I'm not used to having time on my hands.' He paused. 'You have a ride booked for this afternoon, haven't you?'

Lorna's spirits lifted on a faint hope. 'Yes, why? Would you like to join us?'

Martin grimaced. 'No suitable clothes, I'm afraid, though I'd have liked to, very much. It's ages since I had a good gallop. No, I just wanted to check it'd be OK if I stayed round here while you were out. I've a scheme I want to work on...something that occurred to me this morning.'

'Make yourself at home,' Lorna invited him. 'Jane should be here later to open up the shop if you need anything,' she added, with a small niggle of jealousy that it was her friend who would have the pleasure of Martin's company while she, Lorna, was busy elsewhere. Still, it wasn't Jane who had been out to the Galleon, nor been held in his arms beneath the stars...

* * *

It was the shop that was Lorna's first port of call after the ride, and she found Jane there alone, adding up the takings.

'You've had a good afternoon by the look of it.' Lorna grinned, nodding at the healthy pile of notes. 'Had a lot of customers?'

'Heaps,' Jane replied cheerfully. 'I don't remember a busier time ever.' She stowed away the money and locked the till. 'In fact, I was run off my feet till Martin came and lent me a hand, and I must say he's a born salesman. A couple had been dithering for ages over whether to buy one of my bracelets, and he not only got them to buy that, but a ring and a scarf as well. We could do with him here more often.'

Amen to that, Lorna agreed silently, but merely smiled. 'That's great,' she said. 'So where is he now? Back in the house? He said he had work to do this afternoon.'

Jane frowned. 'I think I saw him go off into the garden somewhere. He told me he wanted to have a look round. Oh, and by the way,' she called out as Lorna was halfway through the door, 'you've got a couple of bookings for the night, and supper's at my place this evening—the three of us. OK?'

'Lovely, thanks.'

Out in the yard, Lorna hesitated. Should she go in and wash and tidy up, or look for Martin?

Even while she was trying to make her mind up, his tall figure appeared by the gate leading from the stable-yard into the garden beyond, and she walked over to join him.

'I should apologise for the weeds,' she said ruefully, 'but there's not much point. I know the garden's gone to rack and ruin, but there is a limit, even for me.' She grinned, noting the mocking light in the deep blue eyes.

'Really?' Martin murmured with gentle irony. 'I am surprised!'

Lorna decided to ignore this and went on, 'I do keep the vegetable patch more or less cultivated—hence the beans and spuds the other night—and Fiona's brother gives me a hand with the mowing, but otherwise...' She shrugged. 'Mum would be horrified if she could see it.'

There was a short silence while they walked side by side along the overgrown path, then Martin stopped, his eyes narrowing as they wandered over the lawns to the long beds of tangled roses and beyond them to the banks of shrubs and herbaceous plants.

'There's a lot of land here, isn't there?' he commented slowly. 'And you've the paddocks as well...' He pursed his lips, frowning at some private speculation of his own. 'I'm not sure whether you realise it,' he said at last, seeming to weigh his words with more than usual care, 'but you're sitting on a gold-mine here.'

Lorna leant down to pull at a clump of couch grass growing out of the path and looked up sideways at Martin's serious face.

'I'm very pleased to hear it, but as Glenmore's not for sale, it's not going to do me much good, or make my workload any less.' She straightened up, hands on hips. 'And, anyway,' she went on, 'I don't know that you're right. This isn't valuable farming land, or a building plot in Surrey, you know. Just an old family home on not very fertile soil—except for growing weeds.' She laughed and moved off towards the house, assuming that to be the end of the matter, but Martin quickly caught her up.

'I was quite serious, and I do know what I'm talking about,' he said. 'It's not the land as such I'm referring to, but something else entirely. I've had an idea, you see, and I've been working on it ever since this morning. Listen.'

His eyes were bright with an enthusiasm which wasn't to be denied and which forced Lorna to meet his gaze, sharply intent as he began to formulate his scheme. Something told her she wasn't going to like what he had to say, but there was no way he was going to be put off.

'There's no good hotel in this part of the island, is there?' he began, and Lorna shook her head.

'None. But you don't need me to tell you that. You wouldn't have come here otherwise.'

'So I guess a decently run, modern, comfortable hotel would do very well. Nothing too grand, or out of keeping with the area, of course, but with good food and facilities like a tennis court, say, or a putting-green and maybe the use of a nearby loch for boating and fishing.'

Lorna nodded slowly and caught the end of her plait, which had swung over her shoulder, to play with the end of it. 'I suppose so,' she admitted reluctantly.

'A gold-mine,' Martin reiterated, 'as I told you. A small one, but still potentially very profitable.'

He waved his arm towards the paddocks then tucked it into Lorna's almost absent-mindedly. 'You've already got the riding nicely organised, and you could use that spare land either side of your drive to build two or three log cabins for self-catering, like the Forestry Commission's. Still,' he grinned, 'that's looking rather far into the future. The hotel would be our first project.'

Lorna stared at him, open-mouthed. 'The hotel?' she repeated wildly. 'What hotel? You mean here, at

Glenmore? You can't be serious, not after all I've told you about how I feel about it?'

'I don't mean knock it down,' Martin explained impatiently, 'but convert the existing house, extend it, using the same materials—the possibilities are endless. You only said you didn't want to sell it or let it to strangers. My plan would mean you could remain in charge and run the new venture yourself.'

He shook her arm gently and tilted her face up to his. 'You're a very capable woman, Lorna Morrison. I've seen you in action, don't forget, and you're well able to make a great success of something like what I have in mind. And if you had doubts, there are plenty of courses catering for people who want to learn management skills. That wouldn't be any problem. You could go on one while the house was being converted, come to that. Then no time would be lost.'

'And you haven't lost any time, either, have you?' Lorna found her voice at last and pulled her arm away angrily from Martin's possessive grip. 'You've got it all worked out, haven't you? You've got a nerve, I must say.'

'I've only worked out the outline,' Martin said mildly. 'There'd be a thousand details to agree on before we could go ahead.'

'"We"? What do you mean, "we"? And where's the money coming from for your grandiose scheme?' Lorna asked with icy politeness. 'A bank loan? I don't think my bank manager would be too keen to finance me. Or had you some sort of mortgage in mind—or a fairy godmother, maybe?'

'Godfather, actually,' Martin corrected her with another of his infuriating grins. 'It's something I thought I could help with—I and my company, that is. It would fit in very well with our operation, and you'd have ready-made bookings from our tours.'

'You!'

At last Lorna could contain herself no longer and she backed away from him, her eyes flashing emerald sparks of fury. 'You want to buy me out, turn Glenmore into some flashy hotel for your tourists, cover my paddocks with bungalows——'

'For heaven's sake, Lorna,' Martin interrupted her, exasperated. 'You just haven't been listening, have you? Who said anything about flashy hotels? Certainly not me. And it was more of a partnership I had in mind, not a takeover by any means. You'd run it, be in charge, as I said, with my financial backing. You ought to take it as a compliment.'

Lorna's expression did more than any words could have done to inform him what she felt about that remark, and he shrugged.

'Think about it, anyway,' he invited her.

'I have thought about it,' Lorna snapped, 'and it's very kind of you to take such an interest in my affairs,' she went on with heavy irony, 'but I've been managing pretty well up to now, thanks very much, and I dare say I'll go on managing after you've gone back to Glasgow and forgotten all about me.'

She took a step nearer and glared up at him. 'I'm sorry if you've found Glenmore a bit downmarket for you, but I did warn you when you arrived it was no four-star hotel. It was your choice to stay. But there are people, like Mr and Mrs Collins, who actually come here just because it's homely and unpretentious. They're the sort of people I like catering for, not the rich and sophisticated!'

She swung on her heel and set off again along the path, determined to end this discussion once and for all, but Martin still hadn't finished.

'Stop a minute, Lorna. I want to show you something—please.'

With his tall figure blocking her escape there was no alternative, other than an undignified scuffle, to doing what he asked, Lorna realised with annoyance. Why wouldn't he leave her alone? Surely he knew how she felt by now?

'Well?' she asked brusquely. 'What do you want to show me that's so important?'

'All this.'

Martin slipped his arm round her waist and turned her firmly to face back the way they had just come, looking out at the garden and beyond to the hills sheltering the loch where they had parked the evening before, and the rolling moorland she knew so well.

'I have seen all that before,' she said sarcastically. 'And I thought you'd know by now that my one aim is to keep it all as it is, unspoilt and beautiful.'

'And I want you to see it as a place full of wasted potential—in the right hands, of course.'

'*Your* hands, you mean.' Lorna twisted furiously away from him. 'And you're simply not getting them on Glenmore, now or ever. It's mine, and it's going to stay mine, and what's more, I want nothing to do with your precious scheme. Nothing, do you hear?'

'One day you may be sorry you turned down my offer,' Martin said quietly. 'It was made in all good faith, to benefit us both.'

He stood aside to let her pass, his eyes more profoundly blue than she'd ever seen them as they narrowed suddenly. 'You may say you love the place, but, if you really loved it, I'd have thought you'd have jumped at the opportunity to give it a new lease of life. How long do you think you can keep it going as you are now, running it on a knife-edge of profit? What happens if you're ill, or the house needs rewiring, say? Where's the money going to come from then to keep it all going? I tell you, sentiment is all very well, but it has no place in the real world—my world.'

'I'll manage, as I have done up till now,' Lorna snapped. 'And if the real world, as you call it, means ruining all I care about, all this——' she swept her arm round in an all-embracing gesture '—I'd rather keep out of it, thanks.'

She pushed past him, not looking back, and ran into the house and up to the safety of her own room.

'A born salesman', Jane had called him! But Lorna had another, less flattering description for Mr Martin Ritchie. A foot-in-the-door merchant, that was what he was, no better than those seedy little men who came round periodically, trying to defraud helpless old ladies by offering them a pittance for their valuable heirlooms.

Well, she was neither helpless nor old, and she could see only too clearly what Martin was up to. Glenmore, her inheritance, was safe in her hands, and no predator, however plausible, was going to wrest it from them.

Lorna crossed to the window and stared out, wondering where he was now and what he was doing, now that she'd taken the wind out of his sails. There was no sign of him outside and she hadn't heard him come up to his room, so probably he was chatting to Jane . . . Oh, no! Supper!

The last thing she felt like was a cosy threesome in Jane's cottage. She'd have to cry off and leave the two of them together and, she realised, she'd have to tell Jane soon, before she left, or Martin might be stranded here expecting her to give him a lift down to the village.

Despite her drastically altered view of Martin, she couldn't suppress a sharp pang of regret, and a twinge of jealousy too, as she watched Jane's Escort carry the two of them down the drive a little later, without so much as a wave, for what would no doubt be a very convivial evening.

Inevitably Lorna's mind went back to the evening before, but even her memory of that was clouded now by the altercation she'd had with Martin out there in the garden.

How gullible he must have thought her! Lorna paced round the kitchen, unable to settle, furious with herself for falling into the trap of thinking he had been interested, even slightly, in her as a woman.

All she'd been was a convenient companion, someone to amuse himself with and help him while away what otherwise would have been a solitary evening. Then, when he'd judged the time to be ripe, he'd presented her with his master-plan for Glenmore, hoping the wine, the kisses and a few sweet nothings would have softened her up enough to persuade her to fall in with his scheme.

It made her blood boil even to think of it! Her first estimation of him hadn't been far out, after all. He might not be the man behind the holiday village idea, but what he wanted to do was almost as bad, and to her home, too!

Wait till she told Iain—*then* he might change his views. Her eyes softened as she sank on to a chair, only to jump up again almost immediately. She'd go and see him now, this minute. Her old friend's calm, reassuring presence was just what she needed to help her get things into proportion again after the emotional disturbances of the past couple of days.

But Iain, too, seemed to have something on his mind, and certainly wasn't his usual cheerful and equable self.

'Oh, Lorna,' he said with a preoccupied sort of half-smile as he opened the door. For a split second she had the feeling he was almost disappointed to see who it was standing on his step, but she immediately dismissed the idea as ridiculous as Iain pulled himself together and stood back to let her in, his smile broadening into something resembling his normal expression.

'Come in, Lorna. This is a nice surprise—or do you want something from the shop?'

'No, I came to see you,' she told him, settling herself in one of his shabby old armchairs with a contented sigh. 'I felt—oh, I don't know—restless, up at Glenmore on my own, and in need of company. You don't mind, do you? You weren't going out or anything? Maybe I should have rung first.'

Iain stood looking down at her, his large, solid figure infinitely comforting, and Lorna was almost overcome by a sudden desire to throw herself into his arms for reassurance; but something made her hold back. She wasn't sure, yet, just how much she wanted to tell him about Martin, so instead she curled up her legs beneath her and smiled back at him.

'Tea?' he offered.

Lorna nodded. 'That'd be lovely—thanks.'

'So what's been happening up at Glenmore?' Iain called through from the kitchen. 'Trade good?'

Lorna leant back, listening to the homely sounds of kettle being filled, mugs and teapot set on the tray, and felt her tensions easing away at last.

'Quite good. I've two lots of casuals: a nice couple who want to stay on for a few more nights...' she paused, then went on '...and I've had a guest for a couple of nights whose car broke down. He's over on business, though, not a holiday-maker.'

Lorna was glad that Iain was still safely out of sight, for she was sure something on her face would betray the fact that there was something out of the ordinary about that particular guest; but Iain, bustling in with the tray, seemed not to notice anything odd about her expression.

'That'd be the man with the Mercedes, I suppose? Archie was telling me about it this morning.'

Lorna nodded. 'That's him. Martin Ritchie.'

She took the mug Iain offered her and cupped her hands round it, grateful for its warmth. 'Thanks. This is nice, isn't it? It seems ages since we had an evening together.'

'Mmm.' Iain leant forward, shoulders hunched, and stared blankly into the empty fireplace, his brows drawn together in some private preoccupation.

'Iain?' Lorna watched him for a while then, as no reply seemed forthcoming, she put her mug sharply down on the table beside her, and the sound roused him from his reverie.

'Sorry.' He grinned sheepishly, but his grey eyes remained clouded as they came to rest on her face.

'There's something...' they both said together, and as they laughed Lorna felt the atmosphere lighten.

'You first,' Iain invited her. 'Mine'll keep.'

'I wanted to ask your advice,' Lorna said slowly, 'but maybe this isn't the moment. You've got something on your mind, too, haven't you?'

Iain shrugged. 'As I said, it'll keep. I've waited this long, another few minutes—or days—won't make that much difference.'

Lorna felt a flutter deep in her stomach as she searched his face for the hidden significance of those words, but almost immediately recognised it as a flutter of trepidation, not of joy.

But surely he had been about to propose at last, and, if so, why didn't she feel more elated? After all, this was the moment she had been waiting for for years, a moment that ought to be the happiest in a girl's life, filling her heart with joy, not this sense of relief that he was prevaricating again.

It must have something to do with that upsetting interview with Martin, back in the garden, she tried to reassure herself. It must have unsettled her more than she had realised.

She plucked at the end of her plait and wound it round her fingers.

'Do you ever wonder whether there's more to life than just running the shop?' she asked Iain slowly. 'Wouldn't you like to expand, take on more staff, so that you could get away sometimes—see the world, maybe? Meet more people? Even give it all up and do something entirely different?'

Iain looked startled. 'It's never crossed my mind, and I hardly need to travel to meet people—they come to me, though not as many as I'd like,' he added with a little laugh that, for him, sounded quite bitter, Lorna thought in surprise. 'As for expanding, chance would be a fine thing. It's as much as I can do at present to make ends meet, if you really want to know.' His mouth set into an uncharacteristically grim line. 'That's why I wasn't so dead against that holiday village idea that made you so angry. Anything that would bring in more trade could only be good for me, for Archie, for anyone who tries to provide a service. Even you, I'd have thought.'

Lorna stared at him, appalled, then got up to sit on the arm of his chair and put her arms round him. 'Oh, Iain, I didn't know. Are things really as bad as that?'

'Pretty bad,' he said with a bleak smile that did nothing to reassure her. 'I know how you feel about Mull, and Glenmore, but you have to be realistic, you know. Still,' he shrugged, passing his hands wearily over his face, 'I dare say nothing will come of that particular development scheme. I can't see the powers that be letting it go ahead, and I'll go on muddling along as usual, I expect. I'll manage somehow.'

A silence fell between them, then Iain patted her hand and looked affectionately into her face.

'So what advice were you after?'

Lorna remained silent, staring down at Iain's unruly thatch of brown hair and for a brief, treacherous moment saw in its place another head, dark and disturbingly attractive, and heard again that decisive, almost aggressive voice: 'sentiment...has no place in the real world.'

Martin wouldn't just sit back and hope things would improve. He'd be out there, in his 'real world', touting for business, modernising the shop which still looked much as it had in Iain's father's day—his grandfather's, too, no doubt.

'Well?' As Iain's soft-grained voice broke into her thoughts she shook her head irritably, knowing how unfair she was being, but unable to help herself.

'It doesn't matter.' She got up and went to fiddle with an ornament on the mantelpiece before turning to grin wryly at him. 'Mine'll keep, too.'

Iain laughed. 'That was all very inconclusive, wasn't it? Come on, let's have a dram. You don't have to go just yet, do you?'

CHAPTER SEVEN

IT WAS a couple of hours later that Lorna climbed into the Land Rover to set off for home after the dram, which had been followed by a meal they'd concocted together in Iain's kitchen, laughing and joking like old times.

But it wasn't quite like old times, Lorna thought wistfully as she drove slowly through the village and headed for Glenmore, for, underlying all that easygoing conversation, she had sensed a new strand of anxiety in Iain. There was definitely something on his mind, but whether it was a proposal of marriage or not she was still no nearer finding out. Maybe he'd tell her at the show when he felt more relaxed.

The thought of the island's annual agricultural show, now only a week away, cheered Lorna up considerably, much more than her visit to Iain had done.

That always was a really special day. Shops and offices closed, pubs out of range of the festivities were empty of customers and everybody who possibly could descended on the little village in the centre of the island to have a day out and enjoy themselves to the full.

Iain and Lorna always went together, and this year would be no different.

'You'll be going to the show?' Iain had asked her as he'd seen her out into the street. 'I'll pick you up as usual, shall I?'

'I'd have had something to say if you didn't, Iain MacDonald,' Lorna had retorted with a grin. 'And I'll make the picnic as usual. I'll ask Jane if she wants me to make enough for her, too, shall I? She's got a stall this year, and, knowing her, food will be the last thing on her mind.'

An odd light had flickered behind Iain's grey eyes, just for a second, then it was gone.

'We'll all meet up there, then,' he had remarked lightly, 'if not before, and at the ceilidh after?'

'Of course.'

Lorna had to restrain her feet from tapping against the pedals now at the thought of the ceilidh where they all danced the evening away after the show, and her heart at last lightened only to lurch wildly as ahead of her she spotted a tall figure striding purposefully along the road.

The long northern twilight hadn't given way to darkness, and Martin could have seen his way back to Glenmore quite easily, but Lorna knew she had no option but to stop and pick him up, whatever misgivings she might have about him.

She slowed to a stop beside him and leant across to slide the window open.

'Would you like a lift, Martin?'

'Lorna? What are you doing here? I thought you were back at Glenmore. Jane said you wanted an early night.'

Martin climbed in beside her and slammed the door shut, smiling across at her.

Lorna steeled her heart against his easy charm and put the Land Rover into gear rather more noisily than usual.

'I thought I did,' she said shortly, 'but I changed my mind. I had to go and see someone.'

'A good friend?' Martin enquired casually.

'That's right,' she replied evenly, determined to give nothing away. Her relationships had nothing whatever to do with this man, especially not after he'd revealed himself in his true colours.

'And did you have a pleasant evening with Jane?' she asked.

'Very agreeable, thanks.' There was a pause, then he went on, 'I've seen Archie, and he says he'll have the car ready first thing tomorrow. He'll bring it up to the house after breakfast, so I'll be heading back to Glasgow in the morning.'

Lorna nodded. 'I'll have your bill ready, then.'

They might have been strangers meeting for the first time, Lorna thought with a pang of regret she did her best to stifle, and the evening before might never have happened. She ought to be glad he was leaving so soon, feeling the way she did about his devious attempts to get his hands on her home, hands that had held and caressed her...

But he made no sign of wanting to touch her now. There was no kiss in the shadow of the wall, only a polite goodnight before he made his way up to his room for the last time to pack and disappear from her life for ever.

Soon after breakfast the following day Archie drove the big black Mercedes up to her front door, and Martin deposited his luggage in the hall and went to look for Lorna to say goodbye.

'I'm sorry if I offended you with my suggestions for Glenmore,' he said as he held out his hand. 'And I apologise if I spoke out of turn. It was an honest offer of help, and if you'd felt able to go along with my ideas I do think we'd both have benefited—in several ways,' he added with a gleam in his eyes Lorna chose to ignore. 'And if you ever have second thoughts about my scheme, you have my address. I left it in your visitors' book.'

Against her better judgement Lorna let him take her hand, feeling his fingers tighten round hers as they had done that afternoon when he had arrived so unexpectedly on her doorstep—when was it? Only two or three days ago, but so much seemed to have happened in that short time...

'So it's goodbye, then?'

The pressure of the strong fingers increased as Martin's deep voice broke into her reverie and Lorna looked up at him, green eyes held captive by the penetrating sea-blue stare fixed on her face.

'Goodbye,' she echoed with a faint smile. 'And if I do decide to branch out, you'll be the first to know, but it's not likely, I assure you. Don't bank on any change of heart, will you?'

She steeled her heart against the smile that lit his face as he released her hand.

'I won't,' he promised, 'but there's no harm in hoping, is there?'

During the week that followed it was easier than she might have anticipated to put Martin and his schemes from her mind, for a sudden rush of visitors kept her on her feet from early morning to late at night, when she fell into bed and an exhausted and dreamless sleep.

'I can't ever remember being so busy,' she confided to Iain as she collapsed with a sigh of relief into the passenger seat of his old van on the day of the show. 'I began to wonder how I was going to manage to keep this day free, let alone persuade my guests to move on.' She laughed. 'I know it's the most unbusinesslike thing to do, especially when I could let every room in the house, but show day is sacred, so far as I'm concerned. No visitors, no responsibilities—just fun.'

'Same in the shop,' Iain agreed, 'but I'm not complaining. It's seen the wolf from the door for at least another month or two.'

Lorna turned to grin at him but saw that the words hadn't been a joke. He was in deadly earnest, and the anxiety she'd sensed that evening the week before still lay there behind the grey eyes narrowed against the brilliant light of the sun shining in through the windscreen.

'Forget your worries just for today,' she told him lightly, laying her hand on his arm. 'It's supposed to be a holiday, a time to enjoy yourself. In fact, I think it's just about my most favourite day of the whole year.'

Iain murmured something non-committal as he steered his ancient van over a cattle-grid, wincing at each shudder, and Lorna let the matter drop. There would be plenty of time for him to confide in her later on, if he wanted to.

Although they had set off early, the showground was already busy when they arrived.

Lorna got out of the van and looked around eagerly, savouring the bustle and noise around them almost as keenly as though she were seeing it for the first time.

There was movement everywhere. Excited dogs barked; people were calling out to one another and hurrying in different directions; cattle and sheep of a dozen different breeds were being unloaded into enclosures, protesting loudly at the disruption of their ordered lives, and in the distance Lorna could hear a piper practising for the opening ceremony.

She gazed round happily and caught at Iain's arm. 'Isn't it lovely?' she exclaimed. 'When I said just now I thought it was my favourite day I was wrong. I *know* it is!'

A woman got out of the car next to them and carefully lifted out a pile of cake-tins and a basket laden with jam-pots which she handed to her husband.

'Come away now, Hamish. We haven't got all day. I'll take these, and you bring the basket, and be careful, now. I don't want my jam spread all over the grass.'

She swept off to arrange her exhibits for the produce classes followed by other equally determined ladies bearing an assortment of baskets and containers.

'I'm glad I'm not competing,' Lorna observed as they wandered slowly along in their wake. 'Not against that lot.'

'Or judging,' Iain agreed, grinning at the departing backs. 'More enemies are made and friendships lost over the certificates given out in that marquee than in generations of clan feuds. It takes those ladies months to recover from the injustices meted out to them here—I know. I hear them in the shop.'

Lorna and Iain strolled past the big marquee and towards the line of smaller tents.

'I expect Jane's here already,' Iain remarked. 'Perhaps we should go and find her before we look at anything else. It's the first time she's had a stall, isn't it? And she'll need our support—even if it can only be moral rather than financial,' he added, pulling a rueful face which lightened suddenly as they spotted Jane arranging her wares on a table just inside a tent next to a girl setting up her spinning-wheel.

'Hello, you two.' She smiled. 'Come to see what we're up to? I reckon this is a good spot, don't you? People always stop to watch a spinning demonstration, and I'm hoping I can catch their eye at the same time.'

'I'm sure you will,' Iain said warmly. 'Look at this—it's really beautiful.'

He picked up a small brooch, a delicately interwoven circle of harebells in silver and blue enamel, and held it for a moment in his big hand before replacing it gently on its black velvet cushion.

Jane smiled up at him and some fleeting expression in her gentle brown eyes brought Lorna up sharply. If it weren't such a ridiculous idea, you could almost think it was the smile of a girl in love. Then the look vanished as Jane bent to rearrange the boxes beneath the table and Lorna shook her head even as her hands tightened round Iain's arm. She must have been imagining things.

They chatted for a while, then, as people began to come into the tent, Lorna and Iain wished Jane luck, promising to come back later to see how she was getting on, and wandered out again into the open.

The ground was filling up rapidly now, and the show-ring was full of small children on ponies which they stood and watched for a while before Lorna tugged impatiently at Iain's arm.

'Come on, I want to see everything. Let's go and see the Highland cattle.'

Iain smiled indulgently down at Lorna and let her pull him away in search of further entertainment, but, as the morning wore on, she couldn't help noticing that he became increasingly distracted and withdrawn, and several times she lost his attention altogether, even while she was speaking.

Something was definitely preying on his mind, and it was about time she discovered what it was.

'Time for lunch, I think,' she announced firmly. 'Let's find a quiet spot and have our picnic. I'm starving; I don't know about you.'

Without waiting for Iain's reply, Lorna led the way back to the van, collected the picnic basket and a rug, and found a relatively deserted corner at the far end of the field.

The sounds of the show floated distantly across to them and Lorna spread the rug and flopped down on to it, stretching her legs out in front of her and leaning back on her elbows.

Iain sat down beside her and began methodically unpacking the basket, laying out the packets of food in front of them.

'My word, Lorna!' he exclaimed. 'What's this? Smoked salmon? This is a feast, and no mistake. And a bottle of wine, too?'

Lorna sat up and hugged her knees. 'I thought you looked as though you needed cheering up—and feeding up as well, probably. I'm sure you don't eat properly half the time. You need someone to look after you,' she added innocently, rummaging in the depths of the basket for the corkscrew.

She didn't add that it had crossed her mind as she had assembled their picnic that it could possibly turn into more of a celebration than a mere lunchtime snack, if she was right about a certain matter...

Iain looked at her sharply, but said nothing as he carefully uncorked the bottle.

'One of your father's?' he asked, pouring out two glasses and handing one to Lorna.

She nodded. 'I thought it was a shame to leave it all in the cellar forever, and I'm sure some of it needs drinking. He'd want us to enjoy it, I know.'

She raised her glass and grinned at him over the rim. 'Come on, cheer up. Let's drink a toast. To...'

Her words trailed away as she saw Iain put down his glass untasted, his expression suddenly grave.

This is it, her heart told her with a jump. He really is going to ask me to marry him—now.

Lorna's own face reflected the solemnity of the occasion as she too put down her glass and waited for the words she had been expecting to hear for so long.

'Lorna,' Iain said, reaching for her hand to play absently with her fingers. She could see a pulse racing in his neck, but his voice and eyes were calm.

'There's something I need to know, Lorna. I've been wanting to ask you for a long time, but somehow I couldn't. I wasn't sure how to put it.'

Lorna squeezed his hand and smiled affectionately at his dear, familiar face.

'You are silly,' she told him tenderly. 'Go on, I'm waiting.'

There was no gleam of relief in the grey eyes searching her face, only a darker uncertainty. Iain's anxiety was infectious, making Lorna feel quite nervous herself, but she said nothing more and just went on waiting, still holding his hand tightly.

A butterfly settled on his knee, only fluttering off as he took a deep breath and began to speak in a low, almost hopeless tone.

'I expect you realise the shop isn't doing very well. Most of the year it brings in just enough to keep me going, but it doesn't show any sign of getting any better.' He shrugged as a wry smile touched his serious face. 'And you pointed out yourself that mine isn't a very exciting life.'

A wave of remorse flooded over Lorna. 'Oh, Iain——' she began, but he cut her off with a gentle movement of his hand.

'No, you were quite right,' he observed, 'and that's why...' Again he broke off, but Lorna said nothing as she waited almost breathlessly for him to continue. 'Do you think——' he asked with painful slowness, '—and I do want you to be really honest—do you think that it would be fair to ask someone... someone I love,' he added so quietly that Lorna could hardly hear him, 'to share that dull life with me?'

Lorna couldn't bear the suspense any longer. In a great rush of pity and affection she scrambled to her knees and flung her arms round Iain, hugging him to her and kissing him hard on his mouth.

'Of course, dear, dear Iain! Being fair doesn't come into it. Why haven't you asked me before? You ought to know me well enough to know I don't care how much money you make. I've been waiting years to say yes. Of course I will!'

To her surprise she felt him pull away from her embrace and he looked into her face, almost shocked by her outburst.

'You'll what, Lorna?'

'Why, marry you, of course!'

'*Marry* me? Oh, Lorna! That's not...'

Lorna rocked back on her heels, aghast as much by Iain's appalled expression as by his words, the very last she had expected to hear, and her hands dropped like stones to her sides.

They stared at one another in helpless disbelief, then turned simultaneously as a shadow fell across the rug.

'Martin!'

The colour drained from Lorna's cheeks as she met the veiled blue eyes that must have been witness to the last moments, at least, of the scene between her and Iain.

A sense of utter despair assailed her as she slumped back on to the ground, unable to explain to herself, let alone to this man of all people, what Iain's strange behaviour had meant.

'This is Martin, Iain,' she began faintly. 'He stayed——' She broke off then as she registered Iain's expression of utter desolation. He appeared not even to have heard her as he stared fixedly at Jane, whose small figure Lorna hadn't noticed, hidden as she had been behind Martin's larger frame.

'Aren't *you* going to introduce me to your friend, Jane?' he asked in a voice unrecognisably harsh. 'I don't think we've met.'

Jane's brown eyes widened in an anguish of her own. 'My friend? You mean Martin? He's not . . . well, yes, he is, I suppose. A friend, I mean, but that's all . . .'

She spread her hands hopelessly and Lorna got slowly to her feet.

'This is Martin Ritchie, Iain. He met us both last week when he was a guest at Glenmore. I told you his car broke down, but I wasn't expecting . . . that is, he never said . . .'

She, too, ground to a halt and Martin took charge, speaking now for the first time.

'Jane told me all about the show, that evening I had supper with her.'

Only Lorna saw the look of despair sweep across Iain's face as Martin went on, 'It sounded quite something and, as I had a piece of unfinished business to attend to, I thought I'd come back and see what went on. Only I don't seem to have arrived at what you'd call an opportune moment, do I?' His mouth curved into an ironic smile which failed to reach his eyes. 'I guess it would be best if I made a fairly rapid departure. I imagine you'd rather be on your own just at the moment. I have no wish to intrude.'

Lorna looked up at him, knowing it was up to her to say something, but what could she say to him or to anybody else while such a deep uncertainty hovered in the air around them?

'I don't think it matters,' she said weakly, 'not when you know so much already—as much as any of us, actually,' she ended with a brittle laugh.

Iain had got to his feet now, his pained grey eyes still fixed on Jane, and Lorna knew that this was the moment of truth—she had to know, once and for all.

Ignoring Martin, she laid her hand on Iain's arm, forcing him to turn to her.

'Iain, just now...' Her voice broke and she swallowed hard. 'It *was* marriage you were talking about, wasn't it?'

'Yes, it was.'

'But not to me?'

He shook his head and touched her cheek gently with his finger. 'I'm desperately sorry, Lorna, but I'd no idea that was how you felt about me. I'd give anything not to have hurt you, but you see...'

His eyes left her face and moved to the other girl who was standing as though carved in stone, hanging on his every word.

'You see,' he repeated, 'what I was going to ask you was if you thought there was any hope that Jane was fond enough of me to...'

He faltered and Lorna was saved from having to make any sort of reply by a faint sound which made everybody stare at Jane's transfigured features.

'Iain?' she whispered. 'Oh, Iain!'

She stretched out a hand towards him and Lorna watched her childhood friend cover the ground that separated them with two long strides and clasp Jane in his arms with a passion that left Lorna feeling quite dazed.

She had never imagined that Iain could harbour such fierce emotion, and now she knew why. He was fond of her, and even loved her in a brotherly kind of way, but had never been *in* love with her. It was as simple as that.

Transfixed, she watched the two lovers, lost now in an enchanted world of their own from which she was so firmly excluded, hardly aware of the motionless figure of Martin still standing just behind her, a silent observer of this unfolding drama, until a gentle hand touched her shoulder.

'Come on, Lorna, let's leave them together.'

Martin reached out and passively Lorna let him take her hand, hardly knowing where she was going.

'You're very cold,' he said quietly. 'Come on, I've some whisky in my car. Just the thing for shock.'

Lorna felt her icy fingers being tucked into his warm grasp and followed him, unprotesting, through the lines of parked cars to the edge of the field where the big black Mercedes waited, gleaming conspicuously among the shabbier, older vehicles belonging to the locals.

Martin unlocked it and from the boot brought out a neatly folded rug which he draped round her shoulders, then poured her a generous tot of whisky from a flask in the glove-compartment.

'I never travel without it,' he remarked lightly, watching the colour return to Lorna's pale cheeks. 'You never know when you might be marooned somewhere—or called on to help a maiden in distress.'

Lorna turned wide green eyes on him over the edge of the little metal cup. 'I don't know,' she began, then shook her head helplessly. She didn't know anything except that she felt more miserable and humiliated than she'd ever felt in her whole life, as she waited for him to heap on her the sarcastic remarks she knew she richly deserved.

Hadn't she as good as told him, more than once, that there was no man in her life, and hadn't he seen her only minutes ago fling her arms round Iain and agree to marry him? How could she explain that away?

She sat down sideways on the passenger seat, staring out blindly over the rows of cars, unable to think straight.

'You don't know what?' Martin prompted her, then added in a gentler tone than she'd ever heard him use, 'No, it's all right, you don't have to explain anything—not yet. Though I'm very anxious to know why you kept Iain such a secret, especially when you were so eager to marry him!'

He looked down at her quizzically and Lorna blushed, bending her head so that the thick plait fell over her shoulder on to her hunched knees. Automatically she reached for it to twist the end frantically in her fingers, unaware of the glint in the dark eyes above her.

'I guess this isn't the time to go into that,' he observed, 'so what shall we do now? I came to see the show, and it hardly looks as though Jane can give me the guided tour she promised.' He gave a low chuckle. 'Shall you and I have a look round together?'

'Oh, no.' Lorna shrank further back into the car. 'I couldn't. You leave me here, if you like, and go and have a look on your own—I'll be all right now, but don't make me come.' Her voice rose in desperation as she pictured the eyes of hundreds of people staring at her, and whispering voices spreading the news that Iain MacDonald wasn't going to marry Lorna after all, but her friend, Jane Baxter.

'Poor Lorna,' she heard the voices reverberate in her mind, 'what will she do now? That Iain's a dark horse, isn't he? Always so quiet and springing this surprise on everyone.'

One day she would have to nerve herself to brave their curiosity and pity, but not now, not so soon.

She got slowly to her feet and carefully folded up Martin's rug, placing it on the seat. All she wanted now was to escape back to her home, to Glenmore, and, like an injured animal, tend her wounds in privacy until she felt strong enough to face the world again.

'I'll be away home, now,' she said with a wan smile. 'Thanks for the whisky; I feel much better now. It was just the shock, you see—oh!' She leant back against the car and closed her eyes in weariness. 'Iain brought me,' she said dully. 'The Land Rover's at home.'

Martin walked round to the driver's door and fished in his pocket for the keys.

'In that case, I see I'll have to forgo the delights of the show, for a while at least. I seem to recall that taxis are rather scarce in these parts at the best of times, and, besides, I owe you a lift, don't I? Come on, climb in.'

Lorna leant back in the comfortable seat, watching the familiar landmarks glide by, then switched her gaze to observe Martin from beneath half-closed lids, finding his strongly defined features strangely reassuring as he took command of the situation and of her own actions.

That there would be a final reckoning she had no doubt, for she knew there was no avoiding the questions that would inevitably come. But she could worry about that later, and about how she was going to face Iain and Jane again, once she'd reached home and sanctuary.

CHAPTER EIGHT

WHEN at last Martin drove into the stable-yard Lorna almost fell out of the car in her anxiety to get into the house.

She ran to the back door, fumbling with the key, and breathed deep sighs of relief when she finally reached the familiar comfort of her big kitchen.

Martin followed her in slowly, shutting the door behind him, and went to stand by the window as he watched her collapse into the nearest chair.

She managed a twisted smile. 'I'll be fine now, and thanks for bringing me home.' She paused, adding, 'What will you do now? I've really messed up your day, haven't I? But you still have time to go back and enjoy the show; it's early yet.'

However, Martin seemed in no hurry to leave and settled himself more comfortably against the edge of the draining-board, thrusting his hands deep into his pockets. He was wearing a smart pair of brown cords today, topped by a soft sweater patterned in yellow and tan, warm colours which now seemed inappropriately festive, Lorna thought dismally.

'I don't know I fancy going back, actually,' he commented reflectively. 'And I'm not sure Jane would be all that keen to take me round, and that sort of thing's not much fun on your own.'

He turned to stare out of the window and hummed tunelessly under his breath. 'I imagine all those revelations came as a bit of a surprise, didn't they?' he asked after a while.

Lorna nodded, keeping her head bent. 'To all of us.'

Martin ignored the bleakness of her tone and went on cheerfully, 'Actually, I could do with a coffee, if you could manage it. I had thought I'd eat back there, but events rather took over, so I'm rather hungry.'

He smiled pleasantly at her as though this were a perfectly ordinary day and he'd just dropped in for a chat, Lorna thought wearily as she got up to put the kettle on, and, although all she wanted was for him to go and leave her in peace, she did have to acknowledge it was no fault of his that his plans had been upset so completely. The least she could do was offer him something to eat and drink, and the sooner she did so, the sooner he'd be on his way.

A short time later Martin was sitting at her kitchen table, tucking into a mutton pie and sandwiches, a steaming mug of coffee before him.

Lorna cupped hers in her hands watching him silently.

'You're not eating too? Did you manage to have something before...?' One eyebrow rose as he waved his hand graphically in what he imagined was the direction of the showground.

Lorna nodded and bit her lip, remembering the almost celebratory feast she'd prepared, the bottle of wine Iain had been about to share before she'd made such a fool of herself, now being used to toast Jane and Iain's newly discovered happiness, no doubt.

'That's good.' Martin smiled approvingly at her as he took another bite of his sandwich. 'It's no good being miserable on an empty stomach.'

There was a short silence while he finished eating, then, 'It wouldn't have done, you know,' he went on in exactly the same tone of voice, so that Lorna had no idea what was coming next until the words were spoken. 'It just wouldn't have done at all if you'd married Iain. He just wouldn't be right for you.'

He spoke as companionably as though they were discussing her choice of curtains, and Lorna stared at him open-mouthed.

'And you're an expert, I suppose? How can you say a thing like that? You don't know Iain at all; you only met him just now and then only for a few minutes. And you scarcely know me, either!'

Martin pushed his plate away and leant back in his chair, linking his hands behind his head.

'I know you well enough to understand what you need, Lorna Morrison, and Iain . . . what's his other name?'

'MacDonald,' Lorna told him grudgingly.

'Iain MacDonald is not it. You need someone to challenge you, make you do outrageous things, give you a bit of fun, and I don't think he'd have been able to do any of that.'

Lorna felt her heart begin to race with mounting fury, but Martin pressed on, giving her no time to reply.

'And what did you intend to do, the two of you? Settle down here, I suppose, run Glenmore between you and live out your days on the island?'

'I expect so—and run Iain's shop.'

'A shop!'

Martin gave a shout of laughter and got up to refill his mug, returning to stand looking down on Lorna's furious face from his superior height.

'What's wrong with running a shop? I didn't realise you were a snob as well as . . . as well as everything else.'

Martin perched on the edge of the table and crossed his arms. 'A snob?' He frowned thoughtfully as he considered the word. 'No, I'm not a snob. But you'd be wasted behind the counter of a shop—a sort of general store, I imagine?'

Lorna nodded unwillingly.

'I told you once before, I think, that I can't bear waste—or maybe you've forgotten?'

'What I choose to do with my life—even waste it—is my affair,' Lorna retorted hotly, feeling imprisoned in her chair, but unable to escape from Martin's disturbingly close proximity without it looking too obvious. 'All I've ever wanted to do was live here, and I took it for granted it would be with Iain,' she went on with a catch in her voice. 'I thought I would never need anything—or anyone—else but Glenmore and him, but it never crossed my mind that he didn't feel the same, that he and Jane...'

Her voice broke now, and she turned quickly from her inquisitor to hide her face and the tears that were threatening to spill down her cheeks.

'I don't want to talk about it,' she said despairingly. 'It's nothing to do with you, and I'm sorry if that sounds rude, but it's the truth.'

She waited, hoping that Martin would take the hint and go, now he'd had his say, but instead she found herself starting back as a hand cupped her chin, none too gently, and forced her to raise her head to meet his eyes, like hard blue stones now, with no hint of his earlier smile.

'So why, if you felt so committed to Iain, didn't you tell me about him when I asked you whether there was a man in your life, and when I asked you straight out whether you were spoken for? Here, in this kitchen, as I remember?'

Lorna remembered too, all too clearly.

'Well?' Martin's fingers tightened painfully, making it impossible for her to draw back or look away.

'Does it matter now?'

'I think it does. Either you weren't as sure, deep down, that Iain was the man you really wanted to marry, or else——' his mouth narrowed '—you're a much more frivolous and heartless sort of girl than I took you for.'

His hand dropped suddenly and he got up and went over to his favourite position by the window to stare out, his broad back turned towards her.

'I don't really think you're the type of girl who'll flirt with any available man who comes along just for a dinner date and a few kisses.'

Lorna flushed scarlet. 'No, I'm not,' she protested hotly.

'Then why?' Martin persisted.

Lorna slumped into her chair and cradled her head between her hands, too exhausted to pretend she didn't know what the question was referring to, and without the energy to make a battle out of it.

'I don't know,' she said, her voice low and expressionless. 'I really don't. I don't know what made me say it, and as soon as I had I felt so guilty, but it was too late to go back.'

'And what about going out with me that evening? Letting me kiss you? Did that made you feel guilty too?'

Martin spoke with a harshness that pulled her up short, and swung round to stare fixedly at her.

Lorna shook her head with a mute plea in her eyes, begging him to stop this hurtful probing into the secret recesses of her heart. 'Why do you keep on and on? You know the worst of me now. Aren't you satisfied? Can't you go away now and leave me alone?'

'I might when you've answered me.'

Lorna got up then and pushed her chair back with a grating sound. 'No,' she whispered, 'it didn't.' She raised great haunted eyes on him. 'Will you go now? Please. I want to be by myself.'

'So you can sit and brood and feel sorry for yourself?' Martin nodded. 'Fine, if that's what you want.' He eased back the cuff of his sweater to look at his watch. 'Let's see . . . that'll give you about three hours to get over the worst of your self-pity and change for the dancing. I'll wait for you in the hall, shall I? I take it my room's still free?'

Surely Martin couldn't be serious? This must be a cruel joke of some kind to get his own back for the way she'd deceived him on his previous visit. But one look at his wintry expression told her he was in deadly earnest. He really expected to stay here and take her with him to the ceilidh, and after all she'd gone through!

Lorna backed away, holding out her hand in front of her as though to ward him off.

'I couldn't go to the ceilidh, Martin. Please, don't make me.' All pride had left her now, her defences had crumbled and all she could think of was how she could get away from this man who seemed determined to make her suffer and rub salt into her still very raw wounds.

'You go,' she urged him in an unsteady voice. 'Iain and Jane will be glad to see you, but I couldn't go with you. You can't force me.'

Martin uttered a sardonic laugh. 'You've a lot less imagination than I credited you with. Do you really think they'd want me there playing gooseberry? No, I'm going, and you're coming with me.'

'No, I can't.' Lorna shook her head desperately and turned to escape as quickly as she could through the door and away to the security of her own room, but she wasn't quite quick enough.

With the lithe agility of a great cat Martin slipped round between her and the door, then, with more gentleness than he'd shown up till that moment, he rested his hands on her shoulders, sliding them down until he had her upper arms pinioned, and forcing Lorna to look up at him, her green eyes wide with trepidation.

'Won't you come with me to the ceilidh?' he asked quietly. 'You've got to face the two of them some time, and it will be so much easier if I'm there.'

Lorna bit her lip to stop it trembling. 'It's not only Jane and Iain; it's all the others. Everyone expected me to marry Iain, you see, and they'll all be staring and feeling sorry for me—or laughing behind my back.'

'Of course they won't. No one will even notice you're there. They'll be much too busy enjoying themselves if what Jane told me is true.'

His face softened as his fingers slackened their grip. 'And there's another thing. How do you think Jane and Iain will be feeling? They've got to face you, remember, and that won't be easy. The sooner you all get the first meeting over, the better, and any awkwardness will be so much smoother with a comparative stranger there,' he added with a strange twist of his lips that went unnoticed. 'I'll help all I can.'

'Help?' Lorna flung at him in a tone of withering scorn as she reached for his arms and tore them from hers. The arrogance of the man was unbelievable! 'Ever since you brought me back you've done nothing but stick the knife in and twist it round and round—and you call that help? I don't think you've any idea what I'm feeling. If you have a heart at all, it's made from pure granite!'

Martin's lips tightened into an almost invisible line and he moved away abruptly. 'But you'll come?' he asked harshly.

'Yes, I'll come.' Lorna tossed her plait back and glared at his averted face. 'But don't expect me to enjoy myself. Or help you to.'

'I wouldn't dream of it,' Martin replied quietly as he straightened up to meet her angry gaze, 'but I would be grateful if you could tell me if you have a room. Or shall I try somewhere else?'

'No, you can stay,' Lorna told him ungraciously. 'Your room—the room you had before,' she corrected herself, 'does happen to be free, but you'll forgive me if I don't show you up!'

Now at last he seemed prepared to let her go and watched as she tore out of the kitchen and up the stairs to her bedroom, flinching with a wry smile as he heard the door slam . . . then silence.

Martin nodded to himself with a kind of bitter satisfaction. His ploy had worked—so far. It was fury that possessed Lorna now, an overwhelming rage against one man that, for the moment at least, left no room for the misery that had filled her heart immediately after the shattering events in the showground.

She flung herself on to her bed and pummelled the pillows, so fiercely that they threatened to burst, before burying her face in them.

What she couldn't understand was why she'd let Martin bully her so ruthlessly, allowed him to batter at all her defences until she'd weakly capitulated to his demands. How could any man be so cruel when he knew what she was suffering?

He'd taken shameless advantage of her weakness by sheer brute force, not persuading with sympathetic understanding as Iain would have done.

Iain...

She turned on to her back and stared up at the ceiling, trying to blot out the memory of that passionate kiss that had proclaimed Iain's love to the whole world—love for Jane, and not for her. She couldn't confront the two of them so soon; she'd go down and tell Martin she'd changed her mind... If only she weren't so tired. She hadn't even the energy to cry.

Lorna didn't hear Martin's footsteps pause outside her room a short time later, notice the unlocked door open a fraction, or see the faint smile on his lips as he closed it softly again before going on to his own room at the end of the passage.

It was with a sense of foreboding that Lorna struggled back to wakefulness an hour or so later, unrefreshed and heavy-eyed.

For a while she huddled into her duvet in a vain attempt to blot out the despair she felt enveloping her and put off for as long as she could the inevitable moment when she must get up and prepare for the ordeal that lay ahead.

She neither knew nor cared what she looked like as finally she left her room to find Martin, her heart thudding in quite a different kind of anticipation from the last time she had descended the big staircase for a date with him.

He was waiting for her in the same spot as on that other evening, which Lorna was resolutely keeping from her mind, and she saw him nod his approval as she crossed the floor towards her.

'Very nice,' he said gravely.

'Thank you,' Lorna returned shortly, promptly regretting her acknowledgement of his compliment. The less they spoke to one another the better, so far as she was concerned.

'Listen,' she said frostily, 'I'm not going to the ceilidh with any thought of enjoying myself. The whole purpose is to get the meeting with Jane and Iain over as quickly as possible, and I have no intention of staying longer than is absolutely necessary. If you want to make a night of it, you're welcome. I can get a taxi home.'

Martin raised his eyebrows. 'Even on show day?'

'I'll manage somehow. You needn't worry about me.'

She spun on her heel and strode off to the kitchen to lock up the back door, sensing Martin's eyes on her ramrod-stiff back as he followed her.

'I know this is an ordeal for you,' she heard him say, 'and I do know——'

'If you're going to say you know how I'm feeling, you can save your breath,' she blazed. 'You don't. No one does, and I don't want your pity either, thanks.'

'I don't think you need my pity,' Martin said, 'and I had no intention of patronising you by saying I know how you feel.' He considered her angry face for a minute, then added with an infuriating grin, 'I'd forgotten your dangerous tendency to jump to all the wrong conclusions. You should be careful, you know; it might get you into real trouble one day—if it hasn't already.'

Lorna opened her mouth to deny this accusation, but thought better of it and clamped it shut again. This evening was going to be quite difficult enough without indulging in unnecessary arguments.

* * *

The dancing was already under way when Martin steered Lorna through the crowds in the big marquee, and they almost had to shout their congratulations to the newly-engaged couple.

Grudgingly, Lorna had to admit privately that her partner had been right about one thing, at least. Her fears that she would be the object of everybody's curiosity or pity were totally unfounded. Several acquaintances noticed her arrival and waved cheerily as she came in on Martin's arm, but even her hyper-sensitive antennae could detect nothing odd or out of the ordinary about their greetings.

She let the hubbub wash over and round her as she watched Iain and Jane take their places for a reel, their faces lighting up each time the intricate movements of the dance brought them together, and a great sense of loneliness flooded over her.

'Come on, Lorna, my feet are itching to join in. Look, there's a set that needs us.'

She dragged her eyes back to Martin's but shook her head. 'No, I'd rather not. You go.'

'You can't sit here all evening, being miserable. And you did agree to be my partner, if you remember? A deal's a deal.'

His hand shot out to grasp her so that there was no way she could free herself without an obvious and undignified struggle, and with extreme reluctance she let Martin pull her across the floor, weaving in and out of the dancers till they took their places and launched themselves into the reel.

Although it was already under way, to Lorna's surprise Martin clearly found the steps as familiar as she did herself, and swung her round with an athletic grace that in other circumstances might—would—have called up an instinctive response in her own body, and even now, in the midst of her dazed confusion of mind, she was mortified to find herself catching his eye with a happy grin, quickly suppressed, as the dance came to an end with a chorus of shouts and whoops.

'There, that wasn't so painful, was it?' Martin teased her as they began to walk slowly back to their table. 'You were almost enjoying yourself, weren't you? Here, look where you're going!'

Someone pushed past in a hurry, knocking into Lorna so that she almost fell against Martin, and to her horror she felt something stir inside her as his arm went round her waist where it stayed, firmly and protectively, until they reached the comparative safety of their table.

He pulled out her chair and without thinking what she was doing she smiled up at him, kindling an answering gleam on the dark face. He made no comment, but merely sat back and watched her take a sip of the drink he'd bought for her earlier.

'I suppose you're wondering how it is I'm such an expert Scottish dancer,' he said airily with a self-satisfied grin that Lorna wasn't sure whether to take seriously or not, then, without waiting for her response, he went on, 'but even if you're not, I shall tell you. You have to thank my mother for the fact that I'm not tripping over your feet all the time. She made me go along with my sister to dancing lessons when I was a boy.' He pulled a face that made Lorna smile in spite of herself. 'I didn't half kick up a fuss, I can tell you. Dancing was for girls, you know; anyway,' he went on, moving his chair so that it was so close to Lorna's their knees were almost touching, 'my mother insisted and after a while I actually began to enjoy it, and a lot of what I learned all those years ago seems to have stuck.'

The musicians began to play again and he held out his hand. 'Shall we begin at the right place this time?'

Their eyes met and for a moment Lorna held his glance, but if there was any hidden meaning behind his words she chose to ignore it. She couldn't begin to sort out her emotions as far as Martin was concerned. Enough that she was here, doing her valiant best to come to terms with her new perception of Iain as a good friend and nothing more.

Again she danced with Martin, but as the following reel was announced he and Jane, who had been standing talking together, were dragged on to the floor to make up a set, leaving her alone with Iain.

'Shall we join them?' he invited her tentatively.

'For Auld Lang Syne?' Lorna smiled sadly, letting him lead her across the floor as he had done countless times in the past.

'Don't say that, Lorna,' Iain protested, taking her hand as they waited for the music to start. 'There'll be other times. We'll still see each other, and do things together.'

The three of us? Lorna asked him silently. His innate kindness was making him unrealistic. Things would never be the same again. How could they?

And something else wasn't the same, she realised with a kind of shock as Iain's strong arm went round her waist. Firm and familiar his embrace might be, instinctively guiding and supporting her through the steps for he, too, was a good dancer, light on his feet for such a big man; but *his* arm didn't arouse the sensations that Martin's had, setting up that disturbing tingle down her spine she'd begun unwillingly to register. Nor did Iain's smile make her heart beat faster; not any more. With Iain she might have been dancing with a brother.

Horrified by her discovery, she pushed these thoughts to the furthest recesses of her mind and concentrated fiercely on the intricate steps, and when the dance came to an end they stood in the centre of the floor, isolated briefly from the rest of the crowd by a lifetime's shared experiences.

Lorna squeezed Iain's hand, feeling an answering pressure in his fingers.

'I'm very glad for you, Iain, and I hope you'll be very happy, the two of you.' She smiled ruefully. 'I don't know how I was so blind. Anyone can see you were meant for one another.'

Iain's grey eyes searched for Jane, brightening as he saw her chatting to a group of people near the bar.

'As long as I can make her happy,' he murmured, then paused, his face clouding in an anxious frown. 'This morning, Lorna,' he began awkwardly, 'I'd no idea, honestly, what you were feeling, and I'd have given anything not to have hurt you like that. You do believe me, don't you?'

Lorna reached up and kissed him gently on the cheek. 'Of course I do, and, as I said, I can't imagine why I didn't see what was happening. But we can go on being friends, can't we—all of us?'

They looked at one another, smiling rather sadly as they each realised things would never, *could* never, be the same between them. A chapter in both their lives had closed, Iain's at least with a happy ending, but as for Lorna's...

Work was supposed to be a cure for unhappiness, and she had plenty of that, and her beloved Glenmore, to keep her occupied.

She watched Jane's face light up as Iain went back to join her, and all at once the fatigue she'd been keeping at bay since her arrival with Martin swept over her.

As soon as she got a chance she whispered to Martin, 'I think I'd like to go home now, but if you want to stay I'm sure I can get a taxi from somewhere.'

The lines of Martin's face softened almost imperceptibly as he took in Lorna's sudden pallor, heightened only by two hectic spots of red high on her cheekbones and the unnaturally feverish brightness of her eyes.

He nodded. 'You wouldn't like one more dance?'

Even though she was sitting down Lorna's legs felt like lead and she looked across at him helplessly. 'You stay,' she repeated, 'I'll be OK.'

But Martin was already on his feet and holding out his hand to her. 'Come on. *I'm* taking you home. After all, I was responsible for bringing you here, and I've never deserted a partner yet.'

He pulled Lorna to her feet and, after saying their farewells to the other two, led her by the hand towards the exit.

Their departure coincided with a lull in the dancing and now Lorna was aware that heads were being turned in their direction—girls' heads mostly—casting admiring and envious glances at her escort and her.

At any other time she might have enjoyed the thrill of being accompanied by such a tall, handsome man, but now she felt too tired to care. All she wanted to do was get home as quickly as possible.

The journey passed in a kind of daze as far as she was concerned, and Martin had to rouse her from a dull torpor when he drew to a halt back in Glenmore's deserted stable-yard.

'Home?' she murmured, struggling into an upright position, and peering muzzily through the window. Martin nodded and reached across to undo her safety-belt.

'Home,' he assured her. 'Out you get; you look half asleep already.'

He escorted her into the house and up the stairs, and Lorna was on the point of opening her bedroom door when she turned to face him.

'Thanks for bringing me home—again,' she said in a low voice, managing a hint of a wan smile. 'I suppose I should thank you as well, for making me go at all. But did you have to be so cruel?'

'Cruel?' Martin asked, astonished by this accusation. 'What do you mean, cruel?'

'Well, unkind, then. The way you bullied me into agreeing to go to the ceilidh, and all those questions you made me answer?' Lorna added faintly as the memory of the scene in the kitchen came vividly back to her.

Martin leant against the wall and looked quizzically down at her. 'If I'd been gentle and sympathetic and put you to bed with a hot-water bottle, it wouldn't have done you any good at all, would it? You'd still have had the ordeal of meeting Jane and Iain ahead of you, instead of which, that's all over. To say nothing of confronting the doubts in your own mind about your feelings for Iain.'

'Doubts? What doubts?'

'You don't need me to tell you,' he said quietly. 'And before you say anything else, don't think I enjoyed it. It wasn't easy, not easy at all...'

His face darkened, then he gave a rueful smile and leant forward to open the door.

'Go on,' he said, pushing her gently into the room. 'Things will look better in the morning, you'll see. What you need is a good night's sleep.'

He bent swiftly to brush her forehead with his lips then, before she could catch her breath, and without looking back, he turned and strode quickly along the passage to his own room.

CHAPTER NINE

BUT sleep simply wouldn't come. Behind Lorna's closed eyelids an action replay of each of the day's sequence of events played itself through with remorseless detail, and if she opened her eyes she could see, imprinted on the darkness of the wall, that appalled expression on Iain's face as she'd flung her arms round him. There was no escape.

She tossed and turned, hearing the big grandfather clock on the landing strike each hour until, at three, she couldn't stand it any longer.

'A drink,' she muttered to herself, flinging aside the crumpled duvet. 'I'll go down and make a drink.'

Maybe a cup of tea would do the trick, and at least just the act of making it was something positive she could do to try to break the web of unhappiness in which she felt herself trapped.

At this dead hour of the night the house felt cold, and Lorna wrapped herself in the big shawl she'd taken to the ceilidh before making her silent way down to the kitchen, where she sat down at the big table to wait for the kettle to boil.

The deep tranquillity of the house enveloped her as comfortingly as her shawl and, as she sat here in the old oak carver that had been her father's, the thoughts and memories that had kept her awake no longer seemed quite so painful.

Life did go on, after all. She would go on running the guest-house, taking people on treks into the hills she loved, and in time the hurt and awkwardness would fade; eventually her life would settle down into some sort of pattern, even if it was different from the one she'd designed for herself as Iain's wife and mother of his children.

The kettle boiled and she made the tea, then sat down again to wait for it to brew.

What was that? A creak on the stair? Lorna smiled. All old houses spoke their little secret sounds in the night, but even as she reached for the milk her hand poised motionless over the jug as she heard the same sound, louder now.

Her heart began to beat faster as she listened, all senses keyed up and targeted towards the hall; then, hearing nothing more, she relaxed with a shamefaced grin. Just her imagination playing tricks.

She poured the tea and cupped the mug between her hands, relishing the warmly solid feel of it, and took a grateful sip. There was nothing as comforting as a hot drink.

There was that sound again! It couldn't just be the stairs. Alarmed now, Lorna put down the mug and was halfway to her feet when the door opened slowly.

'Martin! Heavens, you gave me a fright! What are you doing?'

Martin stood in the doorway, clad only in a pair of pyjama trousers and his yellow cashmere sweater. He didn't answer at once, but came across to the table to pull up a chair close to Lorna's and reached for the teapot. 'May I?'

Lorna nodded and watched as he carefully poured himself a mug and, as she had done, cupped it gratefully in his hands.

'I didn't wake you, did I?' Lorna asked. 'I tried to be as quiet as I could. I didn't think I made any noise.'

The blue eyes gave nothing away as they met hers over the top of his mug. 'I heard you because I couldn't sleep either,' he said, his shoulders moving in a slight shrug. 'I have a few——' he hesitated, frowning '—concerns, let's say, of my own to keep me awake. Something that wouldn't go away.'

'I'm sorry.' Lorna's mouth twisted into a sad little smile. 'That makes two of us. But there's not a lot I can do to help you, is there, when I can't even sort out my own life?'

She stared at the grain in the old table and traced it with her finger, so didn't see the glint in the blue eyes watching her intently.

'I wouldn't say that.'

The words were so quietly spoken that Lorna wasn't sure whether she had heard them correctly, but there was no mistaking the expression—hungry, almost predatory—on Martin's lean face, even half-shadowed as it was in the one dim light.

She drew back in a movement of instinctive self-preservation and pulled the shawl closer round her body, feeling suddenly very vulnerable here, in her night-clothes, with this unpredictable man staring at her so strangely.

She was utterly at his mercy if...

For something to do she stretched out her hand for her mug of tea, but it never reached its target. Strong fingers shot out to cover hers and take them prisoner in a powerful grip that gave her no chance of escape, and a tremor ran up her arm, making her whole body shiver.

'There is something you could do for me.'

Martin's voice was oddly husky and Lorna dared not shift her gaze, keeping it fixed on the fingers of her free hand twisting frantically at the fringe of her shawl.

She shook her head, but Martin chose to ignore her mute signal of denial as his hand moved, stroking her arm with a sensuous caress before slipping beneath the thick woollen folds enveloping her. An involuntary shudder ran through her, communicating itself to the man by her side and she gasped as his other hand reached out and touched her cheek, tilting her face back in his cupped hand so that she found herself, at last, staring directly up at him.

Martin's expression was unfathomable, his eyes watchful and searching, and as Lorna gazed into them it seemed as though the very colour went through a sea-change, deepening to indigo pools in which she was in grave danger of drowning.

She began to say something, but the sound that emerged was inarticulate, more like the cry of some animal, as Martin's thumb slid across her trembling lower lip.

Then, rising slowly from his chair, he dropped his hand to capture the fingers still twisting on her lap and drew her up to face him, forcing her to relinquish her protective hold on her shawl.

A little smile touched his lips as he grasped the two edges of the garment to pull her close, stooping to brush her lips with the softest of kisses that sent another tremor quivering through every nerve of her body.

'You are very beautiful,' he breathed, punctuating each word with another kiss—on her lips, her eyelids, her neck—until the room swam before her half-closed eyes and she swayed helplessly towards him to find herself pressed hard against the unyielding muscles of his chest beneath the deceptive softness of his sweater.

There was no one in the house, no one to whom she could turn for protection against the desire she knew was burning in this man who was still hardly more than a stranger, and yet she knew Martin wasn't the sort of man to take her by force and it still wasn't too late to draw back from the brink—if she wanted to.

The hands that still held her prisoner within her shawl moved suddenly to hold the soft flesh of her upper arms, caressing their nakedness with teasing strokes of his fingers, stealing under them to rest against the swell of her barely covered breasts, and the moment when she might have denied him had gone forever.

Whatever happened now was as much her decision as his, and with a little sigh of capitulation she reached up, almost shyly, to rest her own hand on the back of his neck which stiffened against the touch of her fingers.

'Ah . . . Lorna!' Martin's face contracted as though in pain before his mouth came down on hers in a ferocious assault that left her lips bruised—and aching for more.

She ran her hands down his back and slipped them beneath the soft wool sweater, taken by surprise at her own power to give pleasure.

Martin pressed against her, hard in his need for her, and wordlessly turned her in his arms to walk slowly towards the door.

Lorna's heart pounded against her ribs and her breath came in panting gasps as he led her up the stairs and along the passage where he paused briefly outside her bedroom door, shook his head at the mute enquiry in her eyes, and guided her to his own room.

Lorna, lost in a haze of ecstasy, couldn't even begin to imagine why he had done this, but nothing mattered any longer save the ache of desire overwhelming her senses and the almost convulsive pains surging deep through the most secret parts of her body as he pulled her on to the bed to lie beside him.

Martin propped himself up on his elbow and, with a half-smile playing round his lips, pushed back the tumbled hair from her flushed face.

'Don't look so scared,' he said gently as he gazed into the wide green eyes staring up at him.

Lorna moved her head against the pillow. 'I'm not,' she whispered. 'Not with you.'

Martin's lips curved tenderly. 'Have you never...?' he began, not finishing his sentence, and Lorna shook her head again.

He enfolded her then within the strong circle of his arms. 'I'll not hurt you,' he murmured huskily against her hair. 'Just come with me...'

Lorna's only answer was to wrap her own arms tightly round the hard body pressed against her. With a little laugh of delight Martin stripped off his own sweater then slowly, tantalisingly, slipped the thin straps of her night-dress over Lorna's shoulders, pushing the flimsy garment down... down, until her body lay revealed to him in all its nakedness.

She tensed instinctively as his hands roamed over her limbs... her stomach... and then her breasts which he kissed in turn, teasing the peaks into burning life with the soft caresses of his lips.

Lorna heard a moan escape her. The pains of desire throbbing through her veins were unlike anything she had ever imagined, each moment a sensual delight to be savoured with ecstatic impatience in anticipation of the next.

Deeper and deeper she sank into a dark ocean of oblivion in which the only sound was that of their uneven breathing, the only movement the waves of passion bearing her inexorably along until, with a cry of mingled agony and joy breaking into the night, Martin claimed possession of her.

They lay locked in one another's arms, not speaking, each melted into the other's being until, at last, they drifted into the sleep that had eluded them earlier.

It was light when Lorna woke, still enfolded in Martin's embrace in a blissful state of semi-consciousness, her face lying against his shoulder.

She found she was close enough without moving to touch him with her lips, feeling her breasts swell against him with a new onrush of desire at the masculine tang of his skin. Her stomach contracted with a yearning that broke into Martin's dreams and made him stir beside her. With a feather-light touch she moved her hand along the inside of his thigh, rejoicing in the hardness of the muscles that tensed to her fingers even as he slept.

She looked long and tenderly into his face, the taut lines softer now, the sensual mouth gentler in repose.

His dark hair lay in unruly locks across his forehead and black lashes curved against his cheek, making her want to cry out at the sheer male beauty of him and in longing for the rapture that they had shared but which she knew might never be hers again.

For with the dawn came the harsh realisation that what had happened between them last night had been merely the result of the chance meeting of two people brought together by circumstance—but she wouldn't even think of that now.

Instead, very cautiously, she allowed her thoughts to drift back over the events of the day before which, she discovered with a slight shock, had already taken on a kind of remoteness.

Would Iain—could he, indeed—have been able to rouse her to the heights of passion she had experienced in Martin's arms? she wondered. Even at the ceilidh she'd discovered that it was Martin who caused a stirring in her senses she'd never felt with Iain, however fond she'd been of him. Physical passion had never been a part of their relationship.

A profound sigh escaped her. Why did life have to be so complicated?

The slightest of movements by her side made her turn her head to find Martin smiling at her. He drew her closer to kiss her, then put a finger on the little lines creasing her forehead.

'You shouldn't frown, honey,' he chided her. 'Aren't you happy?'

A radiant smile told him what he wanted to know. 'Very, very happy,' Lorna breathed, and this time her sigh was one of pure contentment. 'And I like it when you call me "honey".'

'And I like your honey-coloured hair . . . and your sea-green eyes,' he added, kissing each in turn. 'And the freckles on your nose. And in fact,' he went on, his own eyes deepening to pools of darkest blue as they lingered on her face, 'I find the whole of you utterly and completely desirable.'

Never moving his gaze, he pushed away the bed-clothes and ran his hand lightly down her body, causing her to shiver uncontrollably as it caressed each swell and curve before finally coming to rest gently on her breast.

Lorna dared not move for fear that the slightest tremor would make him take his hand away. The whole of her body seemed centred on the sensations aroused by the weight of his hand possessing her softness.

His lips came searching for hers and for long, rapturous minutes they lay together, mouth touching mouth and body touching body, until the distant sound of a horse's whinny reminded Lorna that another world still existed outside the four walls of this room.

'I'll have to get up soon,' she murmured against his shoulder. 'I may be in a guest-room, but I'm still supposed to be in charge here.'

'Not altogether.'

With a swift, almost savage, movement that took her by surprise, Martin rolled over to pin her beneath him so that she was imprisoned beneath the urgent power of his body.

'You can't keep me here all day,' she murmured as she placed her hands on either side of his head to pull it down to hers.

'I don't see why not,' Martin commented several minutes later. 'It's a very comfortable bed, and we have a lot of sleep to catch up on, to say nothing of getting to know one another better.'

He slipped his hand under her back to press her even closer to him and instinctively Lorna found herself responding to his newly aroused ardour before she turned away to push unconvincingly at his chest.

'Please, Martin, I do have to get up. There are things I must see to.'

'What things?' Martin's lips teased at the hollow at the base of her neck, then, far away, like a sound from another world, the telephone began to ring.

'There you are. I told you.'

'Leave it,' Martin murmured lazily. 'It can't be anything urgent. Not as urgent as this...'

Again he began to cover her with kisses, but with a great effort of will Lorna rolled away from him, grabbing at her nightdress lying on a heap on the floor and pulling it hastily over her head.

'Business is business,' she retorted tartly, looking down at Martin and quelling a desperate urge to fall back into his outstretched arms, 'and, whatever you think of my rather amateur enterprise, I'd have thought you'd have appreciated that.'

'It's all a question of priorities,' she heard him call after her as she sped downstairs in her bare feet, and the first of those will be an answerphone, she told herself, lifting the receiver.

'Yes?' she said breathlessly. 'Glenmore House. Lorna Morrison speaking.'

'Lorna, is that you? You sound a bit peculiar. It's Fiona here.'

'Oh, Fiona.'

Lorna slumped on to a chair and pulled a face. If she'd known, she'd not have bothered.

'Lorna?'

Lorna pulled herself together and tried to concentrate. 'Sorry, Fiona. Yes, I'm fine.' Very fine, she grinned happily, very fine indeed. 'I had to run to answer it, that's all. What can I do for you?'

'Could you do without me today? There aren't any rides booked, are there? It's just that Alec wants me to go over to Oban with him today. Actually, I think he feels guilty about not taking me to the ceilidh last night. Discos are more in his line, and we had a bit of an argument.'

Fiona rattled on, explaining about the row she'd had with her boyfriend, and Lorna let her mind drift happily back to the room upstairs till a silence on the other end of the phone told her that Fiona was waiting for some sort of response.

'You go to Oban with Alec, Fiona. There's nothing on today, and I can see to the ponies. No trouble. Have a good time.'

Nothing on today, Lorna thought with a spurt of joy. Nothing at all. The whole day was free to spend with Martin. Perhaps they could go for a ride together and then... She wrapped her arms round herself to prevent the happiness bubbling up inside her from escaping. After all that had happened yesterday, it all seemed too much.

All at once she realised how cold she'd got sitting in the hall in her bare feet and with nothing on but her flimsy nightdress, and she padded over to the hooks by the front door where there was an assortment of old jackets, and a thick sweater which she slipped on, giggling at her reflection in the hall mirror. Hardly seductive, she thought, but that hardly seemed to matter now.

She paused at the foot of the stairs, suddenly feeling ravenously hungry. Neither she nor Martin had had much to eat the day before, and perhaps lovemaking did strange things to your appetite? It wasn't something she'd had any experience of—till now. It wouldn't do any harm to put some coffee on to filter, then it would be ready when they decided to come down.

She had her back to the kitchen door, so it wasn't until Martin was halfway across the floor that the soft sound of his bare feet on the stone flags made her catch her breath and swing round with a gasp.

'I wish you wouldn't keep doing that!'

'Doing what? This, do you mean?'

With one long stride Martin reached her and drew her close, pressing his mouth to her parted lips and smiling down into her bright eyes.

When he gave her a chance to breathe, she leant back in his arms and touched his mouth with her finger.

'No, not that,' she said, almost shyly. 'Giving me frights was more what I had in mind. Stealing up on me like that. It wasn't fair.'

'I began to wonder where you'd got to. I didn't think a booking would keep you away from me for that long, and I began to imagine all sorts of things—even an assignation with a secret lover!'

'No such luck,' Lorna retorted, 'and, in any case, I don't think I could cope with more than one at a time.'

'That's good.'

Martin made as though to enfold her in his arms once more, then held her away from him to run his eyes over her strangely clad form. He chuckled deep in his throat.

'You don't look exactly sexy in that outfit, if I may say so. But I know what's inside, don't I? And that most definitely is very sexy.'

He thrust his hands inside the baggy sweater, roving over the curves of her body until they reached the warmth of her breasts.

Lorna caught at his fingers and held them to her, conscious of the pounding of her heart as she melted against him, but now they moved again to push back her tangled hair, coiling it round and pulling her head gently back so that she found herself looking deep into his eyes.

'There's one thing I've been wanting to do ever since I met you,' Martin murmured, burying his face in her honey-gold tresses, 'but I suppose it will have to wait.'

He sighed heavily. 'It's not easy to be patient, but now I know——'

He broke off with a grin.

'What do you know?' Lorna asked, all wide-eyed innocence.

His arms tightened round her and he rested his cheek against hers. 'A lot more than I did this time yesterday,' he said, his lips curving into a gentle smile. 'And I'm not the only one to have made new discoveries, am I? About a lot of things.'

Lorna blushed, but she did not answer his smile. 'Yesterday seems an age ago,' she said rather unsteadily, 'and I don't really want to think about it—any of it—for the moment. In fact...'

She caught at Martin's hands and forced them to release their hold of her, stepping back to distance herself from him. She walked over to the window and stared out with unseeing eyes, and when she spoke it was in a dull monotone that might have belonged to another girl rather than the one who only moments before had been so buoyed up with happiness.

How could she say what was in her mind? Yet she must—somehow.

'What you said yesterday—here—about me being heartless,' she began bleakly, 'about me being the sort of girl who'd throw herself at any man who came along for what she could get out of it——'

'I didn't say you *were*,' Martin interrupted her, but a movement of Lorna's hand warned him he must let her finish.

'Well, if you weren't sure then, I've given you every reason to be sure now, haven't I? Letting you make love to me, and wanting you to——' she added so softly he could hardly hear her '—when only hours ago I was prepared to marry another man. You can't get more heartless, and shameless, and immoral, too, than that, can you? You were right about me, after all.'

There was the sound of a quick movement behind her and then Martin was by her side, taking her in his arms and cradling her to him as though she were a small child in need of comfort.

'You might have been prepared to marry Iain, but you didn't love him, did you? You did have doubts, very serious ones, about that, even though maybe you still couldn't quite admit them to yourself, or you'd never have come to my bed last night—and I'd never have asked you to.'

'No.' Lorna bowed her head. 'You wouldn't, but I——'

'You are *not* that sort of girl,' Martin asserted firmly, lifting her chin with his finger and smiling tenderly down into her eyes now bright with unshed tears. 'You are the most honest, loyal and steadfast girl I've ever met. As well as the most beautiful and desirable.'

'Steadfast?' Lorna echoed. 'I like that, though I'm not sure it's true—or the rest of what you said,' she added with a faint blush.

'I know it is,' Martin countered, then grinned. 'With more cause than most. I could have added stubborn, I suppose, but it wouldn't have been very romantic.'

Then he held her a little away from him, his expression suddenly grave. 'Have I convinced you, honey? It's very important—to me. Use that magic we made last night to banish all your doubts forever.' His arms tightened round her as he went on, 'There was nothing to be ashamed of then—or now—in any way or for any reason.'

He felt her relax against him, and held her close for a long moment before saying in a quite different tone of voice, 'Listen, I brought something for you. I almost forgot, what with one thing and another, but it was really to give it to you that I came over yesterday. The unfinished business I mentioned: the show was just an excuse.'

'Something for me? A present?' Lorna's eyes shone.

'Not really a present—wait there a minute while I go and get it.'

Martin hurried away, leaving Lorna staring after him as wild surmises shot through her brain. Whatever could he have brought her? It couldn't be anything really personal, not after the way they'd parted at the end of his last visit.

Her mind ranged back to the unfair accusations she'd made to this man who she knew now could be so tender and gentle, even as he had claimed her ultimate surrender. How could she have been so wrong about anyone?

'Here it is, Lorna.'

Martin was carrying his briefcase which he put on the table, eyeing her keenly as he opened it.

'I took the liberty of taking some photos when I was here last time, and I showed them to a friend—an architect—and persuaded him to do some drawings. Of course he didn't have much to go on, and he couldn't produce anything detailed, but it'll give you an idea of what *could* be done with Glenmore.'

All the night's joy evaporated into a mist of disillusionment as, with a sickening feeling of *déjà vu*, Lorna sank slowly on to a chair and watched him pull out a sheaf of papers which he spread out in front of her.

Martin flicked a glance across at her stony face and grinned. 'You have a very expressive face, do you know that? But don't jump down my throat till I've said my piece. I know how you love this place—you made your feelings all too clear last time I broached the subject—but just hear me out. Will you do that?'

Lorna nodded unwillingly but said nothing.

'First, then,' Martin went on, 'I want to apologise. I realised when I thought about it that I could have been a lot more tactful in the way I brought the subject up. I must have made it sound as though I'd been uncomfortable here, when nothing was further from the truth. In fact, it was because you made me feel so welcome that I realised your gifts were being wasted on such a small enterprise.'

He searched her face again, but the set lines gave nothing away and he sighed. 'Anyway, I am sorry,' he told her. 'A real bull at a gate, I was, carried away by my own enthusiasm.'

He pulled up a chair close to Lorna's and rested his hand on her knee. 'You see,' he went on, 'the more I think about it, the more I'm *sure* you ought to think seriously about expanding Glenmore, and, when you look at David's plans, I'm sure you'll be as keen as I am.'

He pulled the papers over towards them and held one up for Lorna to see. 'Look, no one would know the house hadn't always looked like that.'

'Except me,' Lorna muttered under her breath.

'He's used all the same materials,' Martin persevered, ignoring her interruption, 'and that extension there——' he pointed at the plan '—although the design is quite modern, he's managed to keep the traditional look as well. What do you think? And take a good look before you say anything,' he added with a wry smile.

'I don't need to look,' Lorna said in a grey sort of voice, 'and I know what I think. I think you've taken advantage of me.'

Martin looked down at her bent head and gave a chuckle. 'I suppose you could say that—and very nice it was, too.' He slipped his hand beneath her hair to stroke her neck, but Lorna pushed it away fiercely and slewed round in her chair to stare at him with a cold fury.

'So you admit it?'

'Admit what?' Martin's smile faded. 'I don't see there's anything to admit to, except my determination to get you at least to consider my idea.'

'No, you wouldn't, would you?' Lorna got up and faced him squarely, holding on to the edge of the table for support. 'But I might have known, mightn't I?'

'Known what?' Martin asked with mounting irritation. 'This is like the riddles of the sphinx—why all these questions? I can't see there's anything mysterious or sinister about what I've done.'

'No, it's all part of a day's work to you, isn't it, wheeling and dealing? You come over here with your "unfinished business", knowing all too well what my reaction's likely to be, but you can't resist having another try. Most people, seeing the confusion we were all in when you arrived, would have had the decency to depart, but not you. You waited to see how the scenario might play itself to your advantage, and sure enough we—I—played right into your hands. Literally,' she ended with a bitter laugh.

'Now, wait a minute!' Martin exploded. 'I did offer to leave, if you remember, and it was you who said I might as well stay. And you weren't too averse to my help, either, were you?'

'I'd have walked home barefoot if I'd known what was going through your mind,' Lorna flung at him.

'And what was that?' Martin's voice was pure steel, making Lorna quail momentarily, but it was too late to stop now.

'As soon as you saw how things were, that my defences were about as low as they could be, you decided that if you played your cards right I'd fall like a ripe plum into your arms. If you used my gullibility and your charm and waited long enough, I'd hand you Glenmore on a plate.'

She raised her head and looked him straight in the eye. 'You took your chance, and you took me, but you're not taking my home as well.'

There was a quick intake of breath and Martin recoiled briefly as though she had inflicted a physical blow on him, but his eyes were blazing now with a ferocity that was almost frightening.

His mouth narrowed to a tight line as he got to his feet with menacing slowness, and stood towering over her.

'I think you must be mad,' he said deliberately. 'Really mad. That's the only charitable explanation I can think of for your obsession with this place. You honestly think I made love to you just to get possession of your *house*?' Sheer disbelief made his voice shake. 'This house? This tatty, crumbling heap of stone?'

His lips curved into a sardonic smile. 'Poor Iain. I hope he realises what a lucky escape he's had. I suppose you expected him to spend all his life helping you prop up this old pile? Scratching a living from the land like all your ancestors—and you had the barefaced nerve to accuse *me* of using *you*!'

'Martin, that's cruel! You've no right to say things like that. You know that wasn't how I felt about Iain.'

Lorna's face was ashen now, but there was no mercy in Martin's expression as he took her chin in his hand and stared down at her.

'You didn't love Iain—not as you might have loved...' His voice trailed off as he looked away for a moment, the lines beside his mouth tightening with some suppressed emotion Lorna couldn't guess at. Then his hand dropped heavily to his side.

'But I'm beginning to realise now that you're not capable of loving anything living, except maybe your horses! Certainly no human creature, no man! All you really love is this building—a building, for goodness' sake!' he repeated with a hoarse laugh. 'Well, I wish you a happy affair together, propping one another up into a lonely old age.'

His hand moved to grasp her shoulder, holding her away from him as he raked her shrinking body with dangerously glittering eyes.

'I don't suppose you'll believe me, and I shouldn't have to tell you, but, to put the record straight, my intentions so far as Glenmore were concerned were strictly honourable.' He laughed shortly. 'I saw—still see—its potential, and yours too, and both are being shamefully wasted, but if that's how you want it...'

His voice dropped but there was no warmth in his tone as he went on, 'I just thought I could show you how you could make something of the place, something worthwhile. And if I had any other motive for wanting to help you—well, I've certainly learnt my lesson, as well as some valuable lessons about human nature. I suppose I should be grateful for that!'

The flow of angry words came at last to a halt, and Lorna stared up at him, white-faced and speechless. Then, without any warning, he seized her arms, pinioning them behind her back and bringing her up hard against his body as he stooped with the swiftness of a hawk to crush her mouth with a kiss so savage that her lips throbbed, bruised and swollen, when he finally released her.

'You said some unforgivable things to me just now,' he said, the arctic brilliance of his eyes matching the chill in his voice, 'so if that's the sort of man you think I am, unscrupulous and only out for what I can get, I may as well give us both the satisfaction of proving you correct.'

He pushed her back, slowly and remorselessly, until she was pinned against the wall, pressing her against the cold stone with his thighs and calling up an agonised response of instinctive desire that Lorna had to summon up every ounce of strength to resist.

Martin's lips and hands explored, caressed and punished every inch of her body till her senses were bludgeoned into a kind of delirium and her legs threatened to give way beneath her, and only then did he let her go, stumbling, back to her chair.

'Stones won't be able to do that to you,' he said harshly as he looked down at her, his features set and grim. 'I hope you have a long and happy life together, you and Glenmore.' He swept his arm round to embrace the kitchen, the house and what he could see of the land outside the window. 'There's clearly no room for me here.'

He strode over to the table and swept up all the drawings and plans and was about to throw them into his briefcase when he paused and pushed them back into a pile.

'They're no use to me,' he said abruptly. 'I shan't make the mistake of coming back. Do what you like with them. If nothing else, they'll make a nice fire to warm yourself by when the nights get long and lonely.'

A cold smile touched the corners of his mouth as he snapped his case shut and he turned to go.

'Martin,' Lorna whispered brokenly, moving her hand in a feeble gesture of despair. 'I never meant... I was wrong, I shouldn't have said those things. Please, don't go.'

Even if he heard her words Martin took no notice, but walked quickly out of the room without so much as a backward glance.

And that was the last Lorna saw of him. She sat huddled and motionless on her chair, transfixed by despair, till she heard Martin's feet running down the stairs almost as though he couldn't wait to get away. Then the front door slammed to and a moment later she heard the car engine start up, wheels skidding as Martin wrenched the Mercedes round. The sound faded as he shot down the drive, then... silence.

CHAPTER TEN

SUMMER turned to autumn and with it came a period of warm, golden weather that brought a new influx of late visitors to the island, keeping Lorna busy and on her feet from morning to night; but even that wasn't enough to fill up the painful void in her heart.

However she fought to keep to the very edges of her mind the memory of a certain man...a magical night...it proved impossible to prevent them creeping into her thoughts, so that each time she heard the sound of a car driving up the track she found herself holding her breath, just for a second, her ears straining for the familiar sound of the Mercedes engine although she knew there was no chance of Martin ever coming back, not after that last scene in the kitchen, those dreadful things they each had said.

But there was so much to remind her of him. Whenever she had to make up 'his' bed, as she would always think of it, for a stranger to sleep in, she would hurry round the room, doing the minimum of dusting, as though pursued by a ghost, fighting back the image of Martin's naked body, his glinting, mocking, tender eyes that would insist on intruding between her and the world of harsh reality.

Once, passing the telephone, she even lifted the receiver and picked up the visitors' book to look up the number Martin had left, only to drop both almost at once. What good would it do to hear his voice? If she did try to tell him how she felt, how deeply sorry she was for the things she had said, he'd never believe her, and why should he?

She'd burnt all possible bridges between them in her stupid, unreasonable defence of her home—and all for nothing. She wouldn't listen when he'd tried to make her see that only a man could give her the warmth and passion—and something more—they'd shared that rapturous night when he'd taken her to his bed. She knew that now, but it was too late. He'd never come back and she'd never see him again.

She tried to maintain a pretence of cheerfulness not only for her guests' sake, but for Iain's and Jane's too, trying to enter into their new-found happiness without letting them catch even a glimpse of her own despair. How difficult it was to hear them making plans for their wedding in the new year, discussing a future together that didn't—couldn't—include her, only she knew.

Even the future of the craft shop seemed uncertain. Although Jane hadn't actually said anything, Iain had a couple of outbuildings behind the shop that could easily be converted into an attractive setting for Jane's work, and there was space for a tearoom too, something that she and Jane had discussed before but had dismissed as impractical at Glenmore with neither of them having time to run it themselves nor the money to pay someone else to do so.

It would make good sense to have all Jane's enterprises in one place, Lorna knew, but somehow she just couldn't bring herself to mention it to her friend. It would be the final nail in the coffin containing all the expectations she'd had for her life and which had been changed so drastically on the day of the show.

It was in the shop one day, when the Indian summer had finally come to an end, washed away by a week of cold, blustery showers, that Jane found Lorna packing away some of the stock for the winter.

She rubbed her hands and blew on them before joining her friend on her knees to help fold up the few remaining scarves into a box.

'Winter's definitely on the way now,' Jane commented, pulling a face. 'And I don't suppose we'll see many more visitors now—oh, that reminds me! I've got some news for you, unless you've heard already?'

'I won't know unless you tell me.' Lorna grinned, rocking back on her heels.

'Well, rumour has it that those developers you got so steamed up about have changed their minds about the holiday village. Too far off the beaten track, or something.' She peered closely at Lorna to gauge her reactions. 'So you can stop worrying about that.'

Lorna's mouth tightened as her eyes flicked to the spot where Martin had been standing that day she'd accused *him* of being connected with that development.

'I thought you'd be pleased,' Jane commented mildly. 'You were worked up about it at the time.'

'I know, and of course I'm pleased.' Lorna got to her feet and wandered over to a shelf of sweaters and ran her hand down them. One was that same yellow Martin had worn on the day of the show, and automatically her fingers caressed the soft wool before she realised what she was doing and thrust her hand into her pocket.

'It's just that suddenly it doesn't seem all that important,' she said dully. 'Such a lot's happened since then. You and Iain . . . and Martin.'

Jane scrambled to her feet and came over to hug Lorna's sagging shoulders. 'You can't fool me, you know,' she said gently. 'You've been marvellous all this time, pretending to be so happy, but we're your friends, don't forget, Iain and I, and we do understand. Although I don't know what happened between you and Martin, I do know you miss him.'

She waited; then, as Lorna remained silent, she asked tentatively, 'Do you love him?'

Lorna looked at her helplessly. 'I don't know,' she began, then spread her hands in a gesture of submission. 'Yes, I do,' she confessed wretchedly. 'But it's hopeless—he won't come back, not after...' Her voice trailed away and Jane knew better than to press her. Whatever row or argument had driven Martin away so abruptly was not her business.

'What you need is a break,' she said firmly and grasped Lorna by the arms to pull her round to face her, shaking her gently. 'Shut up Glenmore for a few days. I don't imagine there'll be queues of people to turn away, not with the weather like this. Fiona can look after the ponies, and I can take care of everything else.'

'I don't know...' Lorna began, but Jane cut her off before she could start enumerating all the difficulties that lay between her and a few days away. 'Where shall I go?' she asked instead.

'Anywhere. It doesn't matter. Go and see your mother. Edinburgh is always a treat at any time of year. Think of the shops.'

Lorna laughed in spite of her misgivings. 'I could do with some new clothes,' she acknowledged, 'though I can't really afford them. Still,' she added, her face brightening, 'I could use your wedding as an excuse to get a new outfit, couldn't I? And I could get your present at the same time.'

'So you'll go?'

Lorna nodded. 'As soon as I can fix everything up here and get in touch with Mum.'

* * *

'You've lost weight,' Mrs Morrison commented bluntly almost before her daughter had taken her coat off. 'And I'm not sure it suits you. You do feed yourself properly, I hope?'

Lorna laughed and gave her mother a hug. 'I look after myself just fine,' she assured her. 'It's just that things get pretty hectic from time to time. It's not exactly a sedentary life I lead, you know.'

'Mmm.' Mrs Morrison didn't sound very convinced, but Lorna could hardly tell her of the sleepless nights, worse since she'd confessed her feelings about Martin to Jane, or the desperate longing for him that overtook her whenever her mind and body weren't actually numb with exhaustion.

Mercifully her mother changed the subject just then and the danger area was avoided for the time being at least.

'So how's Iain, and Jane? And all my other friends?' Mrs Morrison reached for her knitting and kept her eyes averted from Lorna's face. 'I ought to try to get over some time to see them all, but it's too easy to go on putting it off when you get to my age.'

Lorna grinned. 'Go on, Mum, you're no age at all, and anyway, you'll have to come over for the wedding—no excuse.' She paused. 'That was quite a surprise, wasn't it?'

Mrs Morrison glanced sharply across at Lorna who was staring blankly into the fireplace, twisting the end of her plait, a sign ever since childhood that she was perturbed about something.

'A very suitable match, I'd say,' Mrs Morrison said calmly. 'They'll make a good pair, won't they? Just what Jane needs, someone kind and reliable like Iain. Someone to lean on after all she's been through.'

Lorna nodded, her eyes suspiciously bright.

So that was it, was it? her mother thought. She'd often wondered.

Stiffly she got up and went over to perch beside her daughter and put a comforting arm round her shoulders.

'Is that what's giving you those rings under your eyes, my love? Were you in love with Iain?'

Lorna bowed her head and fiddled with the edge of the cushion. 'I've made such a fool of myself, Mum. Ever since I can remember I took it for granted I'd marry Iain, and at the show, when he started to ask me something—how Jane felt about him, as it turned out——' she said with a hollow laugh '—I thought he was proposing to me.' Her throat constricted and she couldn't go on, but her mother waited patiently, knowing the words had to spill out now.

After a while Lorna resumed the story, the painful scene coming to vivid life even in her flat monotone, and Mrs Morrison's heart ached for her daughter as she relived each moment of the day which had transformed her life so drastically.

'I knew you were fond of Iain,' Mrs Morrison said softly, 'but I'd no idea you were really in love with him. All those years, and I never guessed.'

Lorna wriggled free and smoothed back her hair from her flushed face as she stared miserably up at her mother.

'You didn't guess, because I wasn't.'

'Then why...? I don't understand.'

Lorna shook her head and her mouth twisted ruefully. 'Nor did I. I thought I loved Iain. No, that's not right.' She frowned. 'I do love him, but I discovered, very painfully, that I wasn't *in* love with him. Not the way he and Jane are in love, or...'

Again her words trailed away and the penny very slowly began to drop, but Mrs Morrison decided that her daughter had had enough for the time being. She got up and held out her hand.

'Come on, Lorna, love. Help me get the supper. It's grand to see you again,' she added, hugging her daughter. 'I don't see nearly enough of you these days. I suppose you haven't thought any more about giving up Glenmore and coming to live here in Edinburgh?'

Lorna laughed. 'You never give up, do you, Mum? But, as I said earlier, I manage fine.'

If this wasn't the absolute truth she didn't want to worry her mother or give her the excuse to go on nagging her to leave the island and look for what she insisted on calling a 'proper' job. In any case, what could she do that wouldn't involve a lot of extra training? She simply wasn't qualified to launch into a different career.

'Penny for them?'

Lorna, who was supposed to be peeling the potatoes, grinned sheepishly and dragged herself back to the present.

'Sorry, Mum, I was miles away.' She frowned, then turned to face her. 'What would you think of a plan to extend and modernise Glenmore, make it into a good, small hotel with a tennis court and——' what else had Martin suggested? '—a putting-green? Plus the riding, of course, and fishing on Mr Murray's loch?'

Mrs Morrison looked up in surprise. 'Have you come into some money, child? It sounds marvellous in theory, but it would cost a fortune.'

'But, apart from the financial angle,' Lorna persisted, 'you wouldn't mind changing the place? It would never be the same again.'

Mrs Morrison thought for a moment, then shook her head decisively. 'Best thing that could happen to it, if you ask me, ramshackle old place. I could never understand why you wanted to stay there. But you haven't answered my question—who's going to pay for all this? And where do you fit in, or are you thinking of selling it after all?'

Lorna put down her knife and stared out of the window. 'A man called Martin Ritchie came up with the scheme. His car broke down and he stayed at Glenmore till Archie had fixed it. He's in the holiday business—arranging tours, mostly—and he had the idea of doing all those things I told you about. His company would put the money in, and I'd run it.'

Something in her tone of voice warned Mrs Morrison that there might well be something more to Lorna's relationship with this Martin Ritchie than she was telling her, and her suspicions were increased by Lorna's next words.

'I thought it was a terrible idea and I told him so. And now...even if I changed my mind, I don't think he'd believe me. Anyway, he's not the sort of man to make the same offer after being turned down twice already,' she ended bleakly.

'You could use me as an excuse for getting in touch with him,' her mother suggested sensibly. 'Tell him that after discussing it with me you think his plan has possibilities after all.'

Lorna shrugged hopelessly. 'I don't think it'd be any use. He's a very proud man.'

And it wasn't only male pride which stood in the way of Lorna's happiness, Mrs Morrison thought, looking at Lorna's stubborn chin. Something would have to be done, and quickly.

She waited until Lorna was packing for her return to Glenmore before broaching the subject again.

'You look a lot better than when you arrived, my love. I know you'll say it's none of my business, but I think Glenmore is more of a worry to you than you'll let on, even to yourself.' She smiled. 'Why don't you swallow your pride and tell your Martin Ritchie that you'd like to discuss his plans again?'

'I can't——' Lorna began, but her mother ignored her interruption.

'And I'm not so blind I don't know you're more than half in love with this man. I've no idea what happened between you, of course, and I've no intention of prying, but all I will say is that, if you have the chance to put matters right and don't take it, you'll grow into a bitter woman with only yourself to blame, without the man you love, and probably without Glenmore as well.'

Lorna looked up, shocked. 'Without Glenmore?'

'You'll never be able to keep it going without some financial help, and it may as well be the help of someone you trust—at the very least.'

Her mother's blunt words were still ringing in Lorna's ears when she reached home and there was only one way to escape their tormenting refrain.

Without pausing to reconsider, she went straight to the telephone and dialled Martin's number.

'Enterprise Tours, can I help you?' a girl's voice asked brightly. So it was his business number that he'd left.

'Could I speak to Mr Ritchie, please?'

'I'm afraid Mr Ritchie is away just at present. Is there anyone else who could help you? Or would you like to leave a message?'

'Could you ask him to get in touch with Lorna Morrison of Glenmore, when it's convenient? Tell him... No, just leave it. No other message, thanks.'

There, she'd done it! The die was cast and the matter out of her hands.

She should have asked the receptionist how long Martin was expected to be away, Lorna thought miserably some days later. Then at least she wouldn't be disappointed every time she answered the telephone or went through the post.

But supposing he wasn't still away, and had simply ignored her message? Maybe he had no intention of getting in touch with her again—ever—and who could blame him?

Several times in the following days she found herself pausing near the telephone, tempted to ring the office again to check whether he had actually received her message, but cowardice—or pride—got the better of her and she left the receiver where it was. If he wanted nothing to do with her, she must try to put him out of her mind, finally.

One crisp, bright day at the beginning of November, Lorna decided she'd had enough of chores and simply couldn't bear to spend the day cooped up indoors. She'd saddle up her favourite pony, Ben, take a packed lunch and have a good long ride over the moors, something she hadn't done for weeks.

Just the prospect of it made her feel more cheerful and she even found herself humming as she locked the door behind her and swung herself up on to Ben's back.

'Come on, my lad,' she encouraged him as they clattered out of the yard. 'New horizons, that's what we need.'

The grey Highland pony pricked his ears at the sound of her voice and lengthened his stride with an eagerness that matched her own, making her laugh happily. Who could even contemplate living in Edinburgh—or any other city, for that matter—if it meant giving up all this?

The bracken-clad moors swept away in a haze of browns and blues to the horizon, and as they climbed the hill behind Glenmore she could see the little loch below her, sparkling in the wintry sun and reflecting the pale blue of the sky. It all looked very clear, and very beautiful.

Lorna's heart lifted as Ben carried her along the grassy track at a steady canter. This was the life, and this was where she belonged and where she'd stay, whatever difficulties might lie ahead.

They'd travelled quite a distance by the time Lorna decided it was time for lunch. She hitched Ben to a handy bush and let him graze on the short wiry grass while she settled herself against a dilapidated stretch of wall to have her snack, chatting to him as though he were a human friend.

She brought herself up sharp with a shamefaced grin. 'I'll be turning into a dotty old woman, if I'm not careful,' she told the pony who didn't seem all that bothered by the information. 'Talking to myself and my animals. Still, there's no one to hear me except you, and you don't mind, do you?'

Ben twitched an ear and went on munching, and Lorna leant back against the rough stones, half closing her eyes as she let her thoughts drift away in the pervading stillness. She could almost drop off...

Brrr! Lorna shivered as a sudden breeze reminded her that this was the edge of winter, and it would be easy to get chilled sitting here.

'Come on, Ben. Time to go.'

Lorna scrambled to her feet, packed away her things and remounted the pony who, sensing he was homeward bound, trotted on enthusiastically—so much so, in fact, that neither he nor Lorna spotted the rabbit-hole until it was too late.

'Oh, Ben!'

Lorna slid heavily to the ground as the pony stumbled badly, almost falling to his knees.

'Are you all right? No, you're not, are you?' she exclaimed worriedly as poor Ben limped a few steps then stopped forlornly.

She ran an expert hand down his legs. Nothing broken, thank goodness, just a bad sprain, but they were still a long way from home and they'd have to go very slowly.

'Come on, boy,' she urged him. 'We can't leave you here—gently does it.'

At a snail's pace they began to retrace their steps and they hadn't gone far before, almost from nowhere, clouds began to roll in across the hills heralding a good Scottish downpour.

Lorna gazed round, wondering if there was another way home, one where she'd pass a farm where she could get help or shelter of some kind.

A narrow path led off the main track down through the bracken towards the road encircling the bottom of the hill. That might be her best bet, and at least once they were down there they would be walking on level ground, a lot easier for Ben's strained leg to manage.

With great difficulty she got him down to the road, but by the time they reached it the heavens had opened, soaking them unmercifully as they continued their painful way towards Glenmore.

Head bent against the driving rain, and with all her concentration centred on Ben's painful progress, Lorna didn't hear the car coming up behind her until it had drawn level.

A big, black car, it was, very like... Her heart thudded against her ribs.

Martin. It was Martin.

She watched as the car slowed, saw the flicker of recognition on his face, then, unbelievingly, she realised he wasn't going to stop.

With a movement of one hand that might have been a wave he accelerated away and disappeared round the corner in a cloud of spray.

'Martin,' Lorna whispered brokenly, leaning her face against Ben's solid neck. 'Martin, come back. I need you.'

She stared down the empty road, knowing it was quite useless to expect he might return, but unable to quell altogether a tiny flicker of hope that the realisation she was in trouble might make him turn round and come back.

She waited for several minutes, but eventually even that tiny flame wavered and died. Martin wasn't coming.

'Come on, Ben,' she said wearily. 'Not long to go now.' Only four or five miles, trudging along with a very lame and tiring pony in the pouring rain and with an aching heart.

She was so wet now it didn't seem to matter that tears mingled with the rain running down her cheeks and, in any case, who was there to see? She let all the misery she'd kept pent up over the past weeks pour out through the floodgates, her breath catching on a sob every now and again. She didn't know it was possible to be so unhappy.

It was the horsebox she saw first, trundling into sight past a clump of wind-blown pines, and miraculously it seemed to be slowing as it drew near. Lorna blinked the water from her eyes as she peered into the driver's cab to see whose it was, and waved furiously, willing it to stop and offer help, and her heart lifted as it came to a halt just yards ahead.

'Mr MacLean!' she cried out in relief as the farmer jumped down. 'Oh, I am glad to see you. Can you help us? Poor Ben's sprained his leg, and I don't know if he'll make it to Glenmore.'

Mr MacLean put a comforting arm round Lorna's shoulders and gave her a hug.

'Poor lassie. You've got a wee bit wet too, haven't you, the pair of you?' He grinned. 'Still, we'll soon have you both warm and dry—yon pony, anyway. It might be more comfortable for you in your friend's car.'

'My friend?'

Lorna hadn't seen the Mercedes pull up behind the horsebox, just on the curve of the road, and for a moment she thought she must be imagining things as she saw Martin's tall figure appear apparently from nowhere, holding aloft a large, incongruously bright umbrella.

Her legs trembled and her teeth began to chatter as she watched him come towards her, but her immediate concern must be for her pony.

'Ben...' she began, but the two men took control of the situation and before she knew it the pony was rugged up and being driven away to the warmth of the MacLeans' barn, and she herself had been led as unprotestingly to the big, comfortable car where Martin peeled off her sodden jacket before pushing her gently on to the passenger seat.

Then he reached into the back for his rug which he draped round her chilled body before climbing in beside her. With the merest hint of a grin he opened the glove-compartment.

'Rescuing damsels in distress seems to be becoming a habit,' he observed drily. 'One particular damsel, anyway. To say nothing of providing her with reviving tots of whisky.'

Lorna's wide green eyes had never left his face. 'I thought you weren't going to come back,' she blurted out, and began to tremble uncontrollably, almost spilling the whisky from the little cup in her hand. 'I knew you'd seen me, but you didn't stop...'

Her voice cracked and the words wouldn't come as she gazed mutely at the dark, handsome features she had never thought she would see again.

His eyes, as intensely blue as she had ever seen them, rested enigmatically on her face.

'I saw what was wrong, and I thought the best thing I could do was get help as quickly as possible. No point in stopping to make small talk.'

'"Small talk"?' Lorna repeated weakly. 'What do you mean, "small talk"?'

One dark eyebrow rose slightly. 'You know. How are you? Isn't it a terrible day? Can I do anything to help?'

Lorna huddled further inside Martin's rug at the irony in his deep voice.

'No,' came a muffled voice. 'I suppose there wouldn't be much point in that.' She paused, then added, 'Thanks for going for help. I don't know how I'd have managed if you hadn't.'

There was a short silence, then she asked faintly, 'Were you just passing, or were you...?' She swallowed hard. 'Did you get my message?'

'Only yesterday. I've been away for a while, in the States,' Martin said abruptly. 'I would have phoned, but I had some business in Oban so I thought I might as well come across.'

The chill in Lorna's body seemed to intensify with the ice in his voice.

'Oh, I see.'

'So what did you want to get in touch with me about?'

Nothing could be lost now by telling him the truth—part of it, at least. Wild horses wouldn't drag from her the slightest hint of her real feelings towards him.

'Those plans, the ones your friend drew up?' She looked at Martin who nodded curtly.

'The ones you said you wanted nothing to do with.'

'I know. I was wrong—quite wrong.' Lorna reached for her plait and twisted the end furiously round her fingers. 'I've been doing a lot of thinking, you see...about a lot of things. Is your offer still open? About helping me modernise Glenmore, I mean?'

'I don't know. That would depend.'

'I expect it would,' Lorna acknowledged humbly. 'On a lot of things. On my saying I'm sorry for one, and making you believe me.'

She searched his face, noting its lines taut and set as he stared back at her.

'Those dreadful things I said to you,' she stumbled on in a voice hoarse with misery. 'I must have hurt you so much. I'd give anything to be able to put the clock back. I *am* sorry—so very sorry,' she repeated almost inaudibly. She saw the blue eyes glint in the gathering gloom and added desperately, 'I can't imagine why I thought you'd take any notice of my message.'

'Can't you?'

A new note she dared not try to analyse sounded in the deep voice that evoked so many memories, and she shook her head, making drops of water fly off her wet hair to fall on to the rug like shining tears.

Martin shifted in his seat. 'I don't suppose you'll believe me,' he said in a voice heavy with bitterness, 'but I'll tell you all the same. I may never get the chance again.'

Lorna hunched further into the rug, her throat constricting at his deliberate choice of words as she waited for what was coming.

'Since that day,' Martin went on slowly, knowing there was no need to explain which day he was talking about, 'there hasn't been an hour when I haven't wanted to speak to you. I've so nearly rung you hundreds of times, and started dozens of letters which I tore up. I knew it would be no use. How could you ever want anything to do with a man so clumsy, tactless, heavy-handed...?'

He stared blindly out of the window, his shoulders rigid and his knuckles white where his fingers clenched on the steering-wheel. 'When I think how I charged in, presenting you with those damned plans just when——' his voice broke on a mirthless laugh '—just when you needed to be loved, not bullied into some hare-brained scheme I'd thought up. And I accused *you* of being obsessed!'

Lorna's lips moved stiffly as though hardly daring to frame the word that had arrowed straight into her heart.

'"Loved"?' she repeated faintly. 'What do you mean, "loved"?'

Her hand crept timidly towards his knee where it rested so lightly that she wasn't sure he knew it was there.

He turned quickly to face her. 'What do you think I mean?'

'I don't know,' she said haltingly. 'I don't know anything any more.'

'You don't know that I love you?' Martin asked harshly. 'That I began to fall in love with you that first evening, in your kitchen? I told myself it was hopeless, because in spite of what you said—or didn't say—I felt there *was* someone important in your life. But even then, and even when you accused me of lying to you over the island development you were so angry about, I couldn't help myself. I had to go on seeing you.'

He paused, his eyes bleak, before going on, 'When I saw you hurl yourself into Iain's arms I thought I'd lost you forever. Then, that night, when we made love, I began to let myself hope again when I thought you were beginning to feel something for me. I wasn't imagining it, was I? There was something between us, something real? Before I killed it with my stupid, crass blundering?'

'No,' Lorna whispered. 'You weren't imagining anything. I did feel something—and I still do. I love you, Martin, you see. More than anything. And you were right all the time. I have been obsessed, as you said, and too blind to see that what I really needed wasn't Glenmore, my precious heap of stones——' she smiled bitterly '—but something much, much more precious.'

There was a short silence, then she went on, 'That's why I left the message, hoping against hope you'd ring. But you didn't, because you thought I wouldn't listen. Oh, Martin, if only you'd known!'

'If I had, I'd have flown back to you from the ends of the earth,' he said simply. 'Nothing, and no one, would have held me back.'

'But you're here now.'

Martin moved so swiftly that Lorna was taken completely by surprise as one arm pulled her close, hard up against his chest, the other hand cupping her face less than gently, tilting it back so she was forced to look deep into the eyes she'd seen so often in her dreams, glittering now with a barely suppressed passion.

His mouth came down on hers as she had remembered it, hard and demanding, and she felt his tongue caress her lips, almost as though he was tasting her, she thought wildly, clutching at him in a fever of ecstasy.

At last he released her, slipping his hand inside the disordered folds of the rug to find and close over her aching breast.

'You're not the only one who wants to turn the clock back,' he murmured somewhere near her ear. 'But perhaps not to the same time?'

Lorna reached up to draw his head down to hers again, feeling her body melt against his, limp with a desire she dared not surrender to, not here—not yet.

'I need to hear you say you forgive me,' she said simply. 'I'd give anything not to have said...you know...' She gestured feebly with her hand which Martin seized and brought to his lips.

'That I made love to you to get my hands on your property?' he prompted her. Spoken so baldly, the words sounded even more terrible than they had in her worst nightmares, and she bowed her head in shame.

'You never considered the possibility that the reverse might have been the truth?' Martin said quietly. 'That I offered to put money into Glenmore and help you run it just to give me an excuse to go on seeing you? No, of course you didn't,' he answered himself, moving his hand to stroke her cheek. 'Once you've come to a conclusion you hang on to it and worry it like a dog with a bone, even if it's totally wrong.'

There was a long silence in which words hardly seemed necessary, broken at last by Lorna, who asked dreamily, 'So what about Glenmore? I did mean it when I said I'd changed my mind about your plans. Will you still help me?'

'Mmm.' Martin appeared to think deeply for a while. 'As I said, it would depend. On the sort of partnership you had in mind, for a start.'

'What do you mean, "partnership"?' Lorna asked, her heart beginning to beat rather faster. 'We wouldn't have to decide that yet, would we? Surely other things are more important?'

'Not to me. You see,' Martin went on, his voice suddenly husky, 'I find you the most tantalising, desirable girl I have ever met, and a purely business arrangement would be out of the question. I simply wouldn't be answerable for my actions if our partnership wasn't something much—much—closer,' he added, emphasising each word with a kiss.

'You mean...?' She didn't dare go on, and heard Martin chuckle deep in the chest pillowing her head.

'I'm very tempted to wait and see what conclusion you've come to this time, but it's too important to take the risk. Before we go into that, though, there's something I've wanted to do ever since I met you, and I don't intend to wait any longer.'

Lorna's heart pounded with a delicious agony as he fixed his eyes on hers, never wavering, and moved his hands to the back of her head. Then, with a deliberate slowness that she could hardly bear for the sensuous response his touch aroused throughout her body, Martin undid her thick plait, unravelling each strand in turn and running them through his fingers as though he were playing with every nerve-end of her being.

When he had finished he spread her hair, still damp, over her shoulders and buried his face in it with a kind of shudder.

Lorna's arms went round him and she leant her cheek on the dark head lying on her breast.

'You'll never cut it off, will you? I want to do that every night after we're married,' he whispered.

'Married?' Lorna echoed weakly, her eyes shining like emeralds. 'Married? You and me?'

'You and me,' Martin said firmly, then grinned wickedly up at her. 'Do you realise what you've just done?'

'Become engaged,' Lorna said happily, forgetting she hadn't actually said yes to Martin's tacit proposal.

'That too,' Martin agreed, kissing his fiancée tenderly on the lips. 'But something else, almost more important.'

Lorna shook her head wonderingly. 'I don't know.'

'For the first time since I've known you, Miss Morrison, you've just come to the right conclusion.'

Only a sheep, huddled against a rock a little way up the hill, was witness to their ecstatic embrace before, totally uninterested, it moved away, leaving behind in the heather only a tuft of wool blowing in the wind.

COMING IN SEPTEMBER

The eagerly awaited new novel from this internationally bestselling author.

Lying critically injured in hospital, Liz Danvers implores her estranged daughter to return home and read her diaries. As Sage reads she learns of painful secrets in her mothers hidden past, and begins to feel compassion and a reluctant admiration for this woman who had stood so strongly between herself and the man she once loved. The diaries held the clues to a number of emotional puzzles, but the biggest mystery of all was why Liz had chosen to reveal her most secret life to the one person who had every reason to resent and despise her.

Available: September 1991. Price £4.99

WORLDWIDE

From: Boots, Martins, John Menzies, W.H. Smith,
Woolworths and other paperback stockists.
Also available from Reader Service, Thornton Road,
Croydon Surrey, CR9 3RU